The light in the room went on and the steady whir of the projector started. In seconds, the pictures of several young men appeared on the screen. Matt was temporarily distracted when Loren Pritchind stood beside him. Pritchind reached down to separate the robe where Matt had drawn it about himself.

"What're you doing?" Matt demanded.

"I must see how you respond to this movie. I must see how long it takes your penis to erect." Loren Pritchind's mood changed drastically. He roughly shoved Matt's arms on the metal armrests of the chair.

"Now, don't think about me," Pritchind ordered. "Watch the screen."

Matt tried to concentrate on the movie. The first several minutes showed the group of young men walking down a country road. Then they left the road to walk back into a woods. Matt watched the pictures disinterestedly.

Then the movie zeroed in on two young men. They embraced and slowly began to undress each other. Then they began fondling each other's sexual organs.

Suddenly, the light in the room was turned on and Pritchind was standing immediately in front of Matt.

"I see you become aroused very quickly," Pritchind said. "Your homosexual tendencies must be extremely strong. I think now we can begin our therapy in earnest."

Gerald Wening

FIRESTORM

Alyson Publications • Boston

Copyright © 1984 by Gerald Wening. All rights reserved. Cover copyright © 1984 by James Hanlon.

This is a paperback original from Alyson Publications, Inc., PO Box 2783, Boston, MA 02208. Distributed in England by Gay Men's Press, PO Box 247, London, N15 6RW.

First edition, September 1984   5 4 3 2 1

ISBN 0 932870 52 X

All characters in this book are fictitious. Any resemblance to real persons, living or dead, is strictly coincidental.

FIRESTORM

1

Noisy chatter filled the high school cafeteria as the lunch period drew to an end. The wall clock said 12:21. Only four more minutes till the warning bell signaling the return to classes.

Matt Justin distractedly listened to the conversation of his classmates.

Marie Wright never took her eyes off Matt.

"My dad said it was trash," a teenager said.

"So did mine. He only read a couple pages. He said if kids read that stuff they'd get dirty ideas and start to talk filthy."

"Aw hell, there ain't nothin' in it. I read stuff lot hornier than that," said a boy called Tom.

A muffled gasp came from the girls in the group.

Marie covered her lower lip with her upper teeth. Her head remained motionless as her eyes darted from one teenager to another.

"Did you read the whole thing? All the way through?"

"Sure! Some parts I even read a couple times," said Tom. "I like the part where Holden tried to figure out whether he should take that hooker to the hotel."

"That's terrible! I don't even want to hear about it," Marie said.

"Hell, that's life," Tom boasted. "There's nothin' in that book you won't find in life."

"It made me think a whole lot," one girl said. "I really felt sorry for that Holden. I think I know what he felt like. That's how I feel sometimes. I wonder if life's really like that outside Willow Glen."

"Hell, yeah," Tom boasted. "Last summer when me and my folks went to the state fair, I even talked to one of those prostitutes. She came up to me at the tractor pull."

Boys' whistles drowned out the muffled gasps of the girls.

"What did she look like? Was she all painted up? Did she really talk to you?"

"Hell, yeah. She asked me if I wanted to have a good time. She asked me if I was over in Vietnam. I guess I looked mature. If I was in the service she said she'd treat me real good. She was even pretty."

"I don't want to hear any more," Marie squealed. "That's awful!"

"Hell, it's just part of life," the boy said.

"I'll bet you're just making up that whole story about meeting that lady at the state fair," another young man said.

"The hell I am!"

"You're only braggin' to make the girls think you're a big man."

"I'm not lyin'," Tom insisted. "Honest to God! I really talked to one."

"Yeah. Talk. No action. Just talk."

Everyone laughed.

"Hell, I never said we did anything. But I talked to her. I really did."

"So, what's going to happen with that book? Will the principal let Mr. Pendleton use that book for English?" Matt Justin asked.

"I don't think so," Marie answered. "Most parents won't even finish reading it. They say it's smutty. My dad won't even look at it. He said he's heard enough about it to know it's trash. Old man Caffrey's one of the few who thinks we should read it."

"Old man Caffrey?" one of the boys blurted in amazement.

"He said maybe it's time people started to listen to us kids. Find out what we're thinking about."

"God almighty, if old man Caffrey thinks we should read *Catcher in the Rye* I hope the world doesn't end tomorrow!"

Everyone laughed.

"What does your old man think?" Someone posed the question to Matt Justin.

"Hell, ain't you got no sense at all?" Tom asked. "You know Matt's dad is in the hospital. He can't be worryin' about any smutty goddam book right now. Can you, Matt? His dad's got more on his mind than some old book."

"How's your dad doing?" someone asked Matt.

"He's OK," Matt answered quickly.

"Well, do we have to write that book report on *Catcher in the Rye* or not? Man, I hate book reports. It's a double suck. First, you got to read the damn book, then you got to write the damn report. Man, I hate to read."

"I don't think we should have to read that book anyway. It's so old," a girl moaned. "It was written almost twenty years ago. I hate that classic garbage."

"Mr. Pendleton said nobody should read the book till the principal and school board gives the go-ahead. If we're lucky we won't have to read any books."

"It'll either be *Catcher in the Rye* by that Salinger guy or something else. My dad said when he was here in high school all the kids had to read *Silas Marner* and my dad thinks we should read it too."

"Did that Salinger write *Silas Marner,* too?"

"Naw. My dad says some man called George Eliot wrote that."

"Mr. Pendleton told me after class that if we don't read Salinger's book then we'll start right away with our unit on Shakespeare."

"Aw, dammit anyway!" Tom complained. "Shakespeare sucks. He really does. He wrote junk. Did you ever hear the way those guys in his plays talk? It almost makes me throw up. I'll bet Shakespeare was a queer."

Everyone laughed.

"My mother said her new sewing machine has been acting queer," one girl added.

All the boys laughed especially hard at that.

"Hell, you don't even know what a queer is, do you?" Tom asked.

"If it's like my mother's sewing machine, it's something that doesn't work right," the girl said.

"Man, you better believe it. A queer's a pervert. Didn't you know that?"

Tom leaned forward and spoke out of the corner of his mouth.

"Last summer at the state fair I saw a little piece in one of the big city newspapers that a bunch of those homosexuals were having a parade in New York. It was an anniversary of when they rioted in some night club called the Stonehouse or Stonehenge or Stonewall or something like that. I showed it to my dad and it just about blew his mind. He said the cops should have shot all those queers right on the spot. Man, he hates queers."

"Did any of *them* talk to you while you were at the fair?" one of the boys joked.

"Hell, no. You won't find any of them around here. My dad said they only hang around in big cities like New York. He said there may be as many as 20,000 living right here in the United States."

Some of the girls gasped at the large number.

"I don't want to talk about it any more," Marie said. "It makes me nervous just hearing you talk about all that sex."

"I'm tired of listening to Tom's baloney, anyway," another young man said. "Man, he knows everything about sex and hookers and queers. Anybody knows that two men can't have sex with each other anyway. It's not natural. Everybody knows that."

"The hell they can't," Tom insisted. "Just what do you think the word sodomy means? Were you sleeping a couple weeks ago during the preacher's sermon on Sodom and Gomorrah?"

For the next five seconds a loud automatic bell drowned out and ended all conversation. Immediately the students began filing out of the cafeteria to resume their education for the day.

The afternoon classes continued as usual.

The following weeks and months did the same.

As the parents on the school board took their turn thumbing through Salinger's *Catcher in the Rye*, the school calendar continued and the controversy surrounding the book died a slow, steady, silent death. With little comment, *Silas Marner* appeared in the classroom.

With the first warm days of spring, the boys hurried home to help with spring planting. On family farms averaging hundreds of acres, the task was not small. The fields had to be plowed and disked and planted, and these necessary chores took everyone's mind off the small paperback book that was now tucked away in the principal's desk drawer. The controversy about the book suffocated to death in that desk drawer.

Mr. Pendleton, the English teacher, did not return to his teaching position in Willow Glen the coming year. Rumor had it that his contract was not renewed, but neither he nor the school board made much comment beyond that. At graduation ceremonies in late May everyone said the appropriate words to Mr. Pendleton. "Excellent teacher." "Sorry to lose him." "Best of luck." "He would be much happier in a large city high school." Everyone was sure of that.

It was traditional in Willow Glen that after commencement exercises, and during the following summer and autumn months, many high school sweethearts married in the village church. This was the custom in Willow Glen and the high school students came to see it as the natural and inevitable course of life.

It was such attitudes as these that accompanied Matt Justin and Marie Wright to their wedding in the village church in the autumn of 1971, and shaped the first years of their marriage in Willow Glen.

2

"Matt. You awake?"

He didn't answer.

"It's almost five o'clock," she said.

He continued snoring softly and she continued leaning against the doorway. With her right hand she brushed the hair off her forehead as she made her way through the bedroom to the window. Apart from the floorboards squeaking under her slippers and the rhythmic ticking of the clock, the house was quiet. She raised the shade and the first hint of daybreak outlined the window frame.

Turning to the nightstand beside the bed, she picked up the clock, pushed the small alarm button on the back, and replaced the clock on the nightstand. Her hand moved to the man's shoulder. His eyes remained closed.

"You awake yet?" she asked quietly.

"H'm."

"It's time to get up."

"H'm."

"Do you hear me?"

"H'm."

She shook her palm on his bare shoulder. Even though her fingers were outspread, her hand touched but a small part of his shoulder.

His eyes opened wide.

"I'm awake."

She continued shaking his shoulder.

"I'm awake," he grumbled. "Let go."

She took her hand off his shoulder but continued standing, staring at him.

"It's almost five o'clock," she said.

"My alarm was set, Marie. Did it go off?"

"I turned it off."

"Why? I would have heard it."

"It's annoying."

"Huh?"

"Every morning and every morning."

"Huh?"

"Listening to that alarm every morning at five-fifteen. It's annoying. Every morning."

"How else am I supposed to wake up?"

"That's why I came in here this morning. So I wouldn't have to listen to that bell."

He closed his eyes, blocking out her constant stare.

"It wakes Greg up, too," she added.

Matt opened his eyes again but avoided looking at his wife. A single white sheet covered his body. He threw it to the side and with both hands began rubbing his chest and stomach. She could hear it. It was a daily ritual when he awoke. She watched as his hands gradually slowed then came to rest on the upper part of his legs. Even though the room was dark, dawn provided a silhouette of his body stretched out on the bed.

Without saying another word, she walked away from the nightstand.

Matt kept his eyes closed. He waited till the sounds of her footsteps faded to the bedroom next to his before he swung his feet to the floor and sat on the edge of the bed.

He was still rubbing his eyes and face as he walked to the window.

The farmyard was shrouded in mist-gray at this time of morning and, as usual, daybreak brought a serenity to the only home Matt ever knew.

The view from the bedroom window didn't change much over the years. The barn needed painting now and the house had started creaking, but the land was the same. The vegetable garden still separated the house from the barn. And the gravel driveway still circled down to the country road.

Looking out the window every morning brought back memories but it wasn't the memories that caught his attention today. It was the sky.

Unusual appearance this morning.

He glanced from the pink clouds above to the distant horizon where the tip of the sun, rising above the black earth, burned blood-red. Rose-red clouds sailed noiselessly toward the horizon.

"Red sky in the morning, all sailors take warning; red sky at night, sailors delight." As a child in Sunday school, Matt heard the teacher trace this rhyme to the Bible. If the ancient saying could be trusted – and from experience, he knew that it often could – this fourth day of July would see violent weather before nightfall. Memory was now vague, but he thought the rhyme was traced to Matthew's Gospel, somewhere in chapter sixteen. He could no longer remember the verse exactly. Those Sunday school classes were so long ago. Their remoteness clouded his memory much as the sky was overcast this morning.

He watched the fiery rays of the sun piercing the clouds on the horizon, and with every second the pink and red and scarlet clouds that covered the sky like a giant, ever-changing kaleidoscope, grew more brilliant. The sun inched higher and higher till suddenly the ruby tint that drenched the sky was consumed by the sun's firestorm. It was as though the sun's fire bleached the redness from the sky and the blackness from the earth. Within moments, the sky assumed its normal early morning hue.

Matt turned from the window and began dressing. He moved quietly as he stepped into his Levis, buckled the belt, pulled a clean white T-shirt over his head, then sat on the edge of the bed to put on his socks and work boots.

The creaking floorboards of the old farmhouse responded to his footsteps and the noise crackled throughout the house even though he tried to walk lightly. He walked down the short hallway toward the bedroom of his wife.

Matt stopped at the doorway and saw Marie's robed figure resting in bed with her back against the headboard. Dawn had brightened the room so that all objects were distinct and he could see that his wife's eyes were open. But Greg was still sleeping soundly in his small bed on the other side of the room.

"Remember?" Marie asked softly.

A puzzled expression crossed Matt's face.

"It's a holiday. The Fourth of July. Remember? I'm taking Greg with me this morning."

Matt rubbed the fingertips of his right hand over his forehead.

"That's right," he said. "I forgot."

An awkward pause followed as Matt stood in the doorway. Finally, as though to satisfy himself, he continued: "I'll get some breakfast. Then get back to the barn. Shave later. It'll take some time to get the equipment ready. Want to change the oil."

"Should I get up?" Marie asked. The words were halfhearted.

"No. No, don't bother. I'll see you and Greg later this morning when you get back." Matt closed the bedroom door and walked to the kitchen.

The early morning routine had become predictable. He rose at daybreak, ate a quick breakfast, started to work outdoors, and saw his wife and three-year-old son only later in the morning. This morning was no exception.

The hours passed quickly and by ten o'clock the sky gave no hint of the ominous storm that appeared so certain at sunrise. By mid-morning the blue sky was without clouds and the sun was beating down on the countryside with a vengeance unusual for so early in July. The air was turning hot and humid – lazy weather for the strenuous activities planned in the village of Willow Glen that day.

The celebration was traditional: in the morning at the village church, a curious blend of patriotic-inspirational prayers and exhortations. In the afternoon, an old-fashioned, family-style picnic at the community park beside the church and then, after dark, the annual fireworks display. For the village officials of Willow Glen the Fourth of July ranked second only to the county fair in importance. Those two events – the Fourth of July picnic and the County Fair in the third week of August – were the highlights of the summer season. They provided the townspeople with plenty of memories until Christmas and pleasant expectations beginning in January.

Few strangers intentionally wandered into Willow Glen. Most discovered, after getting there, that they missed Junction 235 so they would always turn and head back to the Junction. Families living in Willow Glen and the surrounding countryside are native to the area. Most everyone in Willow Glen was born there; and that's where most will die, too. They're a hardy bunch. Independent. And stubborn. The land demands it and their heritage expects it. It is this secluded, out-of-the-way atmosphere of Willow Glen that allows it to keep its sheltered turn-of-the-century simplicity and remoteness.

The isolated homesteads scattered across the valley look more like toys than homes when viewed from the cliff at the edge of Matt's farm. And when sitting atop that cliff and looking down into the valley, one of the first sights that catches the eye is the village church. Last week it was freshly painted. A community project. The elders decided it was a convenient time to spruce up the exterior before the new preacher arrived.

The gently rolling land surrounding Willow Glen is covered in irregularly shaped geometric patterns: the corn is already knee-high, a sure sign of a good harvest if the weather holds out. And the wheat promises to yield a bumper harvest.

Willow Glen rests in a valley and from its rim the eye can see for miles. Matt grew up on this land. So did his parents and grandparents. But they're all dead now. His grandfather taught him about the land, which sections had the richest veins of soil and which the poorest. And from his dad Matt learned to farm: when to plant and how to harvest. In a sense Matt knew the land better than he knew himself. The land never seems to change. The seasons come and go, but those changes are always expected. The land stays the same.

Matt Justin turned the steering wheel on his tractor to cut one final swath through the pasture. Now that the small wildlife had nested and borne their young, it was time to cut the field. Give it a chance to dry for a couple days, then later in the week, bale the cutting. But with that job, he'd need some help.

After cutting the pasture Matt parked the tractor on the west side of the barn, still cool in a patch of morning shade. He turned off the ignition and the sudden silence came as a pleasant relief after the constant roar of the tractor for the past several hours. After his ears became accustomed to the silence he could hear the distant and muted singing of the congregation in the village church. He couldn't make out the words, the church was too far away. But the melody was familiar: "Faith of our Fathers." As a child he had sung it often with the congregation.

He began whistling the hymn softly to himself as he looked down at the crankshaft connecting the bush hog to the tractor. An ordinary mower could never be used in the pasture. He discovered that as a kid. The only way to cut the thick weeds and tall grass is with a heavy-duty bush hog. As usual, after cutting the pasture, the crankshaft was clogged with long strands of grass and stems of weeds. It was one of nature's unending battles with human contrivances.

The continuous motion of the tractor through the pasture provided a cooling breeze for Matt but now that he was off the tractor and standing still, the heat of the July sun quickly brought beads of sweat to his forehead. Before reaching for the knife that was carefully protected within the sheath attached to the belt on his Levis, he pulled his T-shirt over his head and tossed it onto the tractor seat. Cutting the grass from the crankshaft was a sweaty job. An unpleasant task he never did like. And one that always made him hot.

He stood for a moment, hands on hips, looking at the job before him.

At the age of twenty-two, Matt's height had leveled off at a bit over six feet. His bronzed chest and back left no doubt that he spent most daylight hours working outdoors. The work kept his body lithe and trim; farm chores kept his build muscular. Matt Justin was good looking. Many people said so. The All-American Boy: that's what they called him at high school graduation when he was given an award for his work in agriculture.

By the time the '68 Chevy pulled up the lane to the house, Matt had cut most of the weeds and grass from the crankshaft. He glanced in the direction of the car as Marie slammed the door and Greg came running toward the tractor.

"Daddy! Look! See what I got!"

Matt kicked the remaining grass clippings and weeds from the bush hog before he turned and held his outstretched arms to his son.

"Where did you get that?" Matt asked. Greg began waving a small flag. A small American flag.

Greg ran toward the outstretched arms of his father and the three-year-old boy squealed with delight as Matt picked him up and held him high off the ground.

"I got it from the peeker," Greg said.

"Preacher," Marie corrected. "He's a preacher, not a peeker. A preacher prays, a peeker peeks."

Matt took the tiny fingers of his son and held them to his own lips as he let a whistling trill escape between his lips.

"Now, you do it," Matt coaxed his son. "Make the same sound I made."

Matt held Greg's fingers in front of his own mouth. He kept working until Greg uttered sounds that resembled "preacher" rather than "peeker."

Greg, as usual, gloated over the attention he was getting from his father. The boy finally wiggled loose from his father's arms and ran to the front yard where his interest shifted to attaching the small American flag to the handlebars of his tricycle.

"I see the kids still get a flag at church on the Fourth of July," Matt said. "When I was Greg's age that was really something to look forward to."

"I was sorry you weren't there," Marie answered. "I felt foolish alone with Greg – not having you there with us."

"I'd be glad to go if you can tell me how to get all the work done around here. I'm already at it fourteen hours a day now and I can't get caught up."

"Will you go to the picnic this afternoon?" Marie asked. "Or will you stay here? And work all afternoon?"

The tinge of sarcasm was not lost on Matt.

"I plan on spending the rest of the day with you and Greg," Matt answered patiently. "That's why I wanted to finish my work this morning."

Marie turned abruptly and walked toward the back porch.

The small wad of white cotton attached to the screen door – put there to shoo flies away – wasn't doing its job. As Marie opened the screen door a half dozen flies were bounced into motion and they flew into the house as Marie opened the door wide.

Matt came in right behind her. He went directly to the kitchen sink, sprinkled some scouring powder over his arms and began scrubbing the grass stains that smudged his arms and hands when he cleaned the bush hog. After his arms were cleaned he took a wash cloth and quickly wiped it over his shoulders and chest to remove the dirt and dust from the morning's work.

"Do you have to take a bath in the kitchen sink?"

Marie's comment made Matt turn to look at her. The glance was for a moment only.

"Trying to get the grass stains off. That's all."

He replaced the washcloth, walked through the kitchen, and let the screen door rattle shut as he walked to the tractor where he left his T-shirt.

Matt stopped at the tractor to admire his work. As he surveyed the newly-cut pasture he pushed his hands deeply into his pockets. Greg, who had run to his father and silently stood to his left, glanced up at the man, then turned to look at the field. The child pushed his hands into the pockets of the short pants he was wearing, then glanced quickly at his father. Matt kept his thumbs in his pockets but let his four fingers curl over the outside of the denim pockets; Greg carefully manipulated his small fingers into a similar position in his small pockets.

"It won't be long before you run that tractor," Matt said.

"I can't," the boy said.

"Why not?"

"My legs are too short."

Matt laughed. "They'll grow."

"How soon?"

"Couple years."

"How long is that?"

"Not too long."

"Is it longer than from now to the fair?"

"Yes. Lot longer. It's only a month to the fair."

"How long is a month?"

"Four weeks."

"That's so much I get mixed up," Greg yelled.

Matt stood behind the boy and let his large hands gently rest on his son's shoulders.

"When you grow up," Matt said, "you'll wonder how the years went so fast."

Greg turned his head and looked into Matt's face.

"When I get real old," Greg said, "then I'll run the tractor."

As Matt turned to pick up his shirt, he kicked a large clump of dirt stuck on the rear edge of the pan of the bush hog. The clod broke loose and fell apart with the strong pressure of Matt's foot. Greg watched his father walking toward the house, but before following him the boy took his small foot and gave the back of the bush hog a quick kick. The boy jumped on his tricycle as his father walked onto the back porch of the house.

Matt moved through the kitchen and hallway to the bedroom at the rear of the house. He opened the bedroom door and entered before he glanced up and saw Marie standing in front of the closet door.

She had already removed the pink and white, small check housedress she had worn to church. When he entered the room she was taking off her slip. She removed her bra and turned to Matt. Their eyes met in silence.

"I didn't realize you were changing," Matt said.

"It makes no difference."

"I could have waited."

"We don't sleep together," she snapped. "Why should I care if...."

She did not complete the words.

Matt's eyes remained on Marie but he watched with detached indifference. She was a small woman, slightly built. To Matt, her body always appeared frail. But not her disposition. She quickly brushed past him and walked to the bureau in the corner of the room, opened the second drawer from the top, and removed a pair of white walking shorts and a sturdy-looking work-blouse from among the clothes laid neatly inside the drawer.

Matt watched absentmindedly as she dressed for the picnic. For no particular reason he diverted his eyes and slowly walked to the window to stare through the curtains.

"Marie, it can't go on this way. We've got to talk. If you won't talk I'll never know...."

He stopped in mid-sentence; then he changed the subject.

"At least you and Greg get to visit your home next week," Matt said. "Getting away for awhile. Being around your family for a week. You and Greg should enjoy it."

Marie had finished dressing and moved to the bedroom door. She looked at Matt quickly before putting her hand on the doorknob.

"Neither of us was ready for marriage, Matt. It's that simple. You know it. And now, so do I."

Her words were spoken calmly, with a tone of quiet resignation.

"Is that your only answer?" Matt asked. "We weren't ready for marriage?"

"Don't play dumb, Matt."

"I'm not 'playing' anything. I'm trying to talk about it."

"You want to talk? All right, you talk. You can begin by telling me why you ever married me."

"I thought we loved each other," he said.

"Oh, Matt, can't you be more original than that?"

"What's that supposed to mean?"

"Being physically intimate is fine, Matt. But I'd like some emotional intimacy. I'd like to share your life but I feel locked out. We're cut off from each other. Living in isolation from each other's feelings. Can't you see it? If you love me, why don't you ever show it?"

"Show it?" he asked, raising his voice a bit. "You're the one who moved out of the bedroom. Ever since Greg was born, I could count on one hand the number of times we've slept together."

"I'm not talking about sex." She emphasized the last word.

Immediately, she swept her right hand across her forehead and closed her eyes. Several moments passed before she said quietly, "Perhaps my hopes for marriage were too high. I wanted to share my life with someone, Matt, not just my body. My life. Does that make sense to you?"

Matt continued watching Marie but if there was any message coming from his eyes it was one of not understanding her words.

"Don't get me wrong, Matt. All the girls back in high school thought you were gorgeous. Sweet. A catch. I thought so too, then. But you sure don't mean anything to me now. Not anymore."

"The feelings may be mutual," Matt shot back.

Marie glared at Matt.

The mutual stare cooled the short silence between them.

"We made one fatal mistake, Matt. After graduation when all our friends were getting married, we rushed into our marriage too fast. Way too fast. And then Greg came along. Now we're stuck."

Matt didn't answer.

Marie had only said openly what he suspected she had felt all along. The hurt was no less keen but the spoken words confirmed their feelings.

It seemed pointless to say more, so Matt merely stared as Marie gently pulled the door shut behind her. He was left in her bedroom alone.

3

The parking lot was filled with vans and jeeps, cars and pick-ups as Matt drove into one of the last parking spaces beside the church.

"Looks like we're the last ones here," Marie said.

Matt glanced at his wristwatch.

"We're on time," he said. "It doesn't start till two o'clock. Still got ten minutes."

The church together with the preacher's house was nestled on a five-acre parcel of land to the left of the parking lot and the twenty-acre community park bordered by the river was located to the right. The parking area served as a convenient buffer separating the church and park.

Matt, Marie, and Greg made their way between the parked cars to the crowd of people near the park shelter. Greg walked between Matt and Marie, clutching onto his mother with one hand and his father with the other.

The sight of the crowd and the excitement of the picnic caused Greg to pull his parents' arms. He was anxious to get to the picnic and when he saw Marie's parents there was no holding him. He broke away from their hands and ran to Grandfather Wright. The older man stooped to pick up the young child.

"How's my favorite grandson?" Mr. Wright hollered to Greg.

"I helped clean the hog this morning," Greg boasted.

"When did you get hogs, Matt?"

"Greg means the bush hog," Matt explained. "I don't have pigs, hogs, or sows."

"That's a good one," Mr. Wright chuckled as he ruffled Greg's hair. "Here I thought your dad was keeping secrets from me by raising hogs."

"How do you like Greg's new play suit?" Marie asked her father in an obvious effort to change the subject.

Mr. Wright held the child in front of him and let out grunts of approval as he nodded his head. "I don't see how you keep this boy dressed so nice," her father said. "Every time I see him he's wearing better clothes than he wore the last time."

"Where were you this morning?" Marie's father bellowed to Matt.

"Too much work," Matt said. "You've got a couple sons to help you. I do all my work myself."

Though the Justins and the Wrights lived at opposite ends of the county they considered each other neighbors. When Matt's father was still living, the two older men frequently helped each other at harvest time. That's how Matt first became acquainted with Marie.

Matt was about to say something to his father-in-law when someone tapped him on the shoulder. He turned, and the first thing that caught his eye was the sparkling glint of a silver cross on the neckchain of the man facing him.

"I'm the new pastor of the church. I don't think we've met. Renalski's the name. Gordan Renalski. Reverend Gordan Renalski."

The man was slightly built, bespectacled, and somber as a Puritan at a funeral. His eyes were on the same plane as Matt's. When he greeted Matt the palm of his hand was free of calluses and his pale complexion suggested most of his daylight hours were spent inside the parsonage. The top of his head was completely bald but grayish-black hair encircled the back and sides of his head like a medieval monk's. There was a distinct formality about the man that even his attempts at spontaneity could not disguise.

"My name's Matt. Matt Justin."

"I don't remember seeing you at the worship service this morning. Were you ill?" the preacher inquired.

"No. I guess that... I'm afraid that I had some work to finish," Matt said.

His father-in-law interrupted. "Matt doesn't get to worship service too often. Claims he's too busy."

Reverend Gordan Renalski did not respond to Mr. Wright's comment except to raise his left eyebrow as he examined Matt.

The initial squeaks and squawks from the poorly adjusted amplifying system and the subsequent announcement of the time caused both the preacher and Matt to look away from each other toward the gazebo in the center of the park. A voice over the loudspeaker informed everyone that it was almost two o'clock. Marie with her father and Greg slowly began walking toward the gazebo.

A young man about the same height as Matt came running to the preacher. "Dad, the mayor's looking for you. He wants you to say the invocation at the ceremony." The preacher hurried off and left his son standing with Matt.

Matt was about to move on when the young man spoke.

"My name's Jim. Moved here last week with my parents."

Jim smiled broadly and extended his hand to Matt. The grasp was firm and friendly.

"You live close around here?" Jim asked.

"About five miles away," Matt answered.

"Big farm?"

"Couple hundred acres. Won't get rich. But it keeps me busy."

"Do they carry on this way every year on the Fourth?" Jim asked.

"Sure!"

"Why?"

"That's what they always do."

"Why?"

"It's a tradition."

"Seems dumb. I'll bet most of these people couldn't even tell me what happened back in 1776. Could you?"

Matt ignored the question.

"It's not dumb. It's a tradition," Matt insisted.

"OK. If you say so, it's not dumb," Jim added. "I've just never been to something like this. Reminds me of an old-time movie."

"What else would you do on the Fourth of July?" Matt asked. "Community picnic and fireworks. What else is there to do?"

"Oh, man," Jim laughed. "You're serious, aren't you?"

Matt's eyebrows wrinkled into a frown as he looked at the preacher's son.

The crowd had already assembled around the gazebo and Matt left Jim standing alone on the fringe of the group as he made his way through the people to stand beside Marie and her father. Matt glanced back at Jim and he saw the preacher's son watching him.

The bell in the church steeple rang at two o'clock for the official beginning of the ceremony.

The mayor and the four members of the village council, all veterans of the Second World War, had the annual honor of presenting arms during the brief ceremony. Their spit-and-polish, despite many years and little practice, was bolstered with genuine fervor. With muscles taut and arms rigid, they proudly saluted the flag. The singing of the National Anthem followed.

As the preacher approached the microphone for the invocation, Matt heard a comment from someone behind him.

"Christ, I hope he keeps it short," the voice said. "This heat's strong enough to melt a body."

When Matt turned around to see who made the comment he noticed that Jim had moved around the back of the crowd and had come to stand immediately behind him and Marie and Greg. Jim smiled broadly when Matt noticed him.

Jim tapped Matt on the shoulder.

"Who's that guy? The one leaning on a cane and trying to stand at such rigid attention. Thick glasses. Light green shirt. Gray pants. Who's he trying to impress saluting like that?"

"That's old man Caffrey." The smile vanished from Matt's face as he stared at Jim. "Old man Caffrey had two sons killed in Korea. His third son went to Canada instead of Vietnam."

"Oh." Jim looked down and studied his shoes. "Uh, I didn't know," he mumbled.

Leaves on the trees were motionless. The lack of any breeze and the muggy afternoon air made the heat oppressive as the preacher appeared behind the microphone. But he appeared prim, trim, and proper.

"On this anniversary of our Declaration of Independence," he began, "we thank our Almighty God in heaven for permitting us to be free. And, it is this celebration of freedom that draws us together today. Though many individuals, we are, today, united as one in our celebration of freedom. The Declaration of Independence proclaims what we believe today: 'We hold these truths to be self-evident, that all men are created equal, that they are endowed by their Creator with certain unalienable Rights, that among these are Life, Liberty, and the Pursuit of Happiness. That to secure these rights, Governments are instituted among Men, deriving their just powers from the consent of the governed.' It is this declaration, my dear friends and citizens, that we honor and celebrate today. We enjoy liberty because our forefathers fought for it. Thank God, we live in a country where every human being is free; where oppression is not tolerated, and where all persons are protected by just laws. For this, dear God, we thank You, today and always."

A loud chorus of amens rose from the crowd.

The church choir began "America the Beautiful" and most of the crowd joined in the singing. Matt did not join in the beginning, but only on the last line: "And crown thy good with brotherhood, From sea to shining sea." Willow Glen always typified the idea of brotherhood. It was a close-knit community where conformity was a virtue and individuality was a vice. Matt learned that lesson long ago.

Finally, the mayor led everyone in the Pledge of Allegiance to the Flag. As the assembled group began reciting the pledge Matt said the first lines absentmindedly. It was not until the end of the pledge that he became conscious of the words: "...with liberty and justice for all."

The annual ceremony, without exception, emphasized the same themes: brotherhood, liberty, freedom for all, and justice for every citizen. The ceremonies and the words never meant much to Matt. His work on the farm concerned him more than the abstract speculations he always heard mouthed at these annual picnics. His biggest worry this afternoon was how he could get all the silage from the pasture baled next week.

At the end of the Pledge of Allegiance the mayor stepped to the microphone one last time.

"As mayor of the village of Willow Glen I officially declare the picnic and festivities for this year's celebration of the Fourth of July to be underway."

There was loud clapping and shouting, and someone was already announcing over the loudspeaker that the games were about to begin: horseshoes at the north end of the park; a softball game on the diamond; children's games in the east section; and canoe races on the river. Picnic supper would be served in the church basement about five o'clock.

"Hey, I didn't mean anything before," Jim said.

"About what?" asked Matt.

"Mr. Gaffney. And his sons."

"His name's Caffrey," Matt corrected. "And forget it. You had no way of knowing."

"Were you in Vietnam?" Jim asked.

"Too young. It was almost over by the time I got out of high school. Anyway, I was exempt. My dad just died. I had to take care of the farm."

"Would you have gone?" Jim pressed.

Matt stopped and thought.

"Probably," he answered.

"Why?"

"Civic duty," Matt answered.

"Only ten seconds' thought. Civic duty? You never even thought about it, did you?"

"What's there to think about?" Matt asked.

"Man, I don't believe what I'm hearing!"

Marie, who had been watching the exchange between Jim and her husband, was biting her lip in an effort not to laugh. This strapping hulk of a man was being bombarded with questions from a teenager and the younger was getting the advantage over the older. She finally interrupted.

"I'm taking Greg over to the children's games," she said. "When he gets tired, I'll take him to the shelter and we'll be resting there."

If Jim heard Marie, he ignored her completely. Jim's sole concern centered on Matt.

"Do you play softball?" Jim asked. "They're getting some teams together over at the diamonds."

Matt looked over at his wife quickly. That morning she was so emphatic that she wanted to be with him all day.

"Go on," she urged. "I don't mind."

"Sure?"

Marie was more relaxed this afternoon. Having her father and brothers in sight improved her disposition, and for that Matt was grateful. He watched as she and Greg made their way toward the eastern corner of the park.

"I'll bet you're good at sports," Jim said.

He trailed with Matt toward the ball diamonds.

"Why do you say that?" Matt asked.

"You look like it."

"I can take it or leave it," Matt said.

"If everybody on the team is mediocre, I fit right in," Jim said. "I do even better if everybody on the team is lousy."

"Will you go to Willow Glen High School in September?"

"I'm no kid anymore," Jim protested. "Graduated last month. That's why my dad waited to take up this new church position. It gave me a chance to finish high school in my hometown. Man, I'm glad. Willow Glen is all right and all that, but it's about as dinky as you can get. There's nothing here. A half million people live in the city I came from. Anyway, in September I'll be leaving for college."

Their conversation ended abruptly when they reached the group of men and teenagers preparing to team up for the softball games.

The clouds which appeared at daybreak were gone from the afternoon sky. It remained hot and humid with no sign of rain. The games were played leisurely and really not meant to be won or lost; the afternoon was a convenient way to get together with friends and neighbors – a pleasant break after the hectic schedule of spring planting and the early summer routine of cultivation. It was a day to relax. A day to be with neighbors. The afternoon was one long, organized, social gathering in which all the citizens of Willow Glen got together to gossip. Politely, of course. It was an appropriate, if not altogether unconscious way of preserving the status quo in the community and keeping everyone on the path of righteousness. Fear of gossip, as the residents of Willow Glen learned early in life, has a way of keeping people in line. On the Fourth of July there was little worry of strangers intruding on the closed circle of Willow Glen.

By three-thirty in the afternoon Jim discovered that Matt was as athletically inclined as he suspected; and Matt observed that Jim, contrary to his denial of athletic prowess, was capable and well-coordinated on a ball diamond.

At the end of the game the preacher mingled with the men and made an effort to speak with each individually.

"Win or lose?" the preacher asked.

"Won," Matt laughed.

"I had a chance to talk with your wife earlier," the preacher said. "We talked while you were playing ball."

Matt remained silent but cast a puzzled look at the preacher.

"Marie told me how busy you are. No time for church. Little time for anything except work. She's worried about her marriage."

"Oh?" Matt was careful not to say more. He was more interested in precisely what Marie *did* tell the preacher.

"Your wife needs some of your time, Matt. And your boy does, too. How would you like some help?" the preacher asked.

"With what?"

"Farm chores."

"No... no, I could never ask that," Matt protested. "You've got enough to do taking care of the church business and all. I appreciate your offer but no...."

The preacher allowed his lips to curl in a slight smile and he was about to laugh but he controlled himself.

"I agree. I don't have the time. But my son does. And, he's looking for something to occupy his time."

"Marie may not care for the idea," Matt objected. "She's touchy about any change in routine."

"I already mentioned it to her. I think she'll be agreeable," the preacher said.

Matt answered the preacher after only a few moments' thought. "When you see Jim tell him I'd like to talk with him."

The preacher nodded. "Maybe that will give you enough time to get to church on a regular basis, too. The Sabbath is still the Lord's day, Matt. It should be honored as such."

Matt let the preacher's sermonette go unanswered, but he was encouraged with the prospect of a helper on the farm.

It wasn't long before Jim came running toward Matt.

"My dad told me about the job. Talk about luckin' out! This Fourth of July is turning out super. When can I start?"

"Whenever you want," Matt began. "The work is always waiting, so it's up to you."

Their conversation was suddenly interrupted when a girl with prominent braces on her teeth came up to them and began talking.

"My name's Ellen and my momma and I were watching you play softball. Momma told me you were the preacher's son and that if I asked you, maybe you'd take me for a canoe ride on the river. Momma said she wouldn't worry if I was with you, if you know what I mean. Would you? Take me for a canoe ride, that is?"

"I've never driven a canoe on that river," Jim protested. "We'd both drown."

"You don't drive a canoe," Matt mumbled. "You paddle it."

"Well, I don't know how to do that either."

"Momma said she'd go along and teach us both how to do it. Paddle, that is."

"Too dangerous," Jim muttered, shaking his head. "If the canoe rolled over, we'd get all caught up in seaweeds and river gunk, and I don't think we'd better."

"What do you mean? River gunk? What's gunk?" Ellen persisted.

"Gunk – you know – dead fish, slimy branches, turtle poop – that kind of crap."

"Oh," Ellen said.

"You don't want to fall in river gunk, do you?" Jim asked.

"No," Ellen said. "And I don't think you and Momma should ever sit in the same canoe. She gets a funny look on her face when people use certain words – and you use a lot of them. I don't care how you talk, but I think Momma would. If you won't take me for a canoe ride, how about taking a walk? Momma says since you're the preacher's son she trusts you and...."

Jim interrupted.

"Afraid not, Ellen. I can't do anything with you because... because...."

"Because," Matt broke in, "I'm taking Jim out to my farm right now to show him the work he'll be doing for me. Maybe some other time, Ellen."

Ellen screwed up her nose, widened her lips, and exposed her braces in a peculiarly repulsive show of disgust.

"Maybe we can go for a walk when you get back," she said.

"Now that's an idea," Jim answered.

Ellen's face brightened considerably at the prospect and she ran to tell her mother the good news.

Jim began laughing as soon as Ellen was out of earshot.

"Thanks for getting me out of that one," he said.

"Don't get me wrong," Jim said as he and Matt began walking through the park. "I'm sure Ellen's a nice person but for chrissake! I really mean it! Are all the girls in Willow Glen like Ellen? She acts like she's never been around boys. Did you hear that? Momma this and Momma that. Aw, I really mean it, for chrissake. I can't believe it."

"You sure made an impression on her," Matt teased.

Jim ignored the comment.

"Ellen sat with a bunch of her girlfriends during the ballgame," Matt said. "I didn't realize it till now, but they all had their eyes on you."

Matt kept looking sideways and laughing at Jim's encounter with Ellen.

"Were you serious?" Jim asked.

"About what?"

"Going out to your farm right now to check it out?"

"I was serious."

Jim turned to face Matt but he began running backwards as he called out.

"I promised my dad I'd set up some folding chairs and tables in the church basement. You won't leave without me, will you?"

"You're the only reason I'm going back to my farm," Matt laughed.

"Hey, that's right," Jim yelled as he ran farther away from Matt.

"Give me fifteen or twenty minutes. I'll be right there."

Matt continued laughing as he watched Jim run to the church basement.

"Now," Matt said to himself, "all I have to do is find Marie and see how angry she is."

4

Marie listened as Matt explained the offer made by the preacher and she asked no questions as she heard Matt say how happy Jim was to have the job.

"Did the preacher talk with you?" he asked.

"We had a pleasant chat. He mentioned that his son may be able to help us out. I never thought he'd begin work so soon though. I have the strange feeling that preacher's son doesn't even see me. I guess he knows I'm your wife," she complained. "But as long as he helps with the work, what's the difference."

"Then is it all right with you, Marie?" Matt asked.

"Anything to help get the work done," she answered. "Maybe if you're not so busy, we can work out some other things."

She looked at Matt but his eyes held that same inscrutable expression which she had given up trying to understand long ago. His eyes shifted quickly from Marie to Jim who came running from the direction of the church.

"Ready?" Matt asked.

"Whenever you are."

"We'll be back long before supper," Matt promised. "I'll eat with you and Greg."

Small puffs of white clouds began drifting overhead from the west but they were so small and so widely scattered that they offered no relief from the scorching heat of the afternoon sun.

They weren't out of the parking lot before Jim began talking.

"That river behind the park sure seems tame. It's nice. Peaceful.

Slow. Someday I'd like to explore it. You should have been with me and Willie and four other guys last summer. We took a rubber raft down the Bellashan Rapids. Talk about an adventure. Man, that was it. It took six days. We were on the river most of the morning and early afternoon, then we'd make camp in the late afternoon and sleep out every night. You should have been there. It was great."

"I thought you told Ellen you didn't know how to – what did you call it? – drive a canoe?"

"Aw, I was only trying to be polite. Know what I mean?"

"Then you know how to paddle a canoe?"

"Aw, sure. Canoes, rowboats, rafts, kayaks – you name it. If it floats, I've been in it."

"Know how to swim?"

"Are you joking? I was on a swimming team all four years of high school. Not to brag or anything, but I brought home a couple medals."

"Why didn't you take Ellen out in a canoe?" Matt asked.

"Ellen's not my type," Jim laughed.

"I've got a couple nieces. Marie's brothers are all married and they've got a bunch of teenage girls. Maybe I can fix you up with one of them this summer," Matt offered.

"Hey, get off my back about the girls, all right?" Jim suddenly fell silent and looked out the side window. It was several minutes before Matt spoke again.

"Your father seems like a solemn sort," Matt finally said.

"Oh?"

"Doesn't laugh very much."

"Oh?"

"Does he ever unwind?"

"I guess."

"Are you adopted?"

"What kind of a stupid question is that?"

"You don't act like your father."

"Oh."

"Why do you answer everything I say with 'Oh'?"

Jim laughed.

"I was thinking about the first thing you said. About my father being a solemn sort."

"Oh."

"Now *you're* doing it," Jim said.

They both laughed.

"I guess he isn't funny," Jim said. "I mean he doesn't often laugh. I don't think about it, anymore. But no, I'm not adopted. I'm his biological son."

"Oh."

"There. You did it again," Jim said.

They both laughed.

"He doesn't think life's too funny."

Matt kept driving without answering.

"I do, though," said Jim.

"Do what?"

"Think things are funny."

"Like what?"

"Ellen, for one thing!"

They both laughed again.

"There are other things, too." Jim paused and leaned the side of his head against his upraised arm which he rested on the window ledge of the car.

"What are some of the other things?" Matt asked.

"I enjoy talking with you," Jim said.

"How's that?"

"You listen."

"Everybody does."

"No they don't. They ask questions and they talk a lot but they don't listen."

"I want to hear something funny," Matt said.

"What did you say?"

"You were telling me about things you thought were funny. Tell me one."

"Oh, that's right. Things were funnier when I was a kid."

"Maybe you're growing up. Things get grimmer as you grow older."

"Good God, I hope not!"

"Well, they do."

"Naw, I don't think so. Things are the same for adults as for kids. Don't get me wrong. It's true I may be growing up, but for chrissake, I can't stay a kid forever."

"I want to hear about something funny when you were a kid."

"Hmmm." Jim thought for several moments before speaking.

"You should've heard one of the sermons my dad once delivered. It was funny."

"Your dad's sermon?" Matt seemed incredulous.

Jim laughed.

"You had to be there to know how funny it was."

"Tell me."

"You probably wouldn't think it was funny at all."

"What happened?"

"It's a long story."

"Tell me."

"I was in the eighth grade and it was Sunday morning. The title of my dad's sermon was 'Lord, Where Are You?' He was telling the congregation that whenever they help a stranger, or aid those in need, or do anything for somebody, they're finding the Lord."

"I don't see anything so funny in that," Matt interrupted.

"Well, for chrissake, that wasn't the funny part; that was serious!"

"Oh," said Matt.

"All through his sermon he kept building up to his main point by saying, 'Whenever somebody calls out to us, we hear the Lord.' Then he'd ask, 'Lord, where are you?' Then he'd say it louder, 'Lord, where are you?' Everybody was getting real quiet in church as he kept calling out, 'Lord, where are you?' Well, old Willie Blatz, my buddy – he's one of the guys who went rafting with me on the Bellashan Rapids – was sitting right in front of me with his parents and his older brothers. When my dad reached the high point of his whole sermon, he was yelling real loud, 'Lord, where are you?' And then, suddenly, he stopped talking. You could hear a pin drop. I thought Willie Blatz was whispering something to his mom cause he leaned over, but old Willie left a fart you could hear all over the place. It didn't just whistle like when you first get up in the morning. It rattled the whole bench. Well, Willie started to snicker, then his brothers started, and pretty soon, I was laughing so hard I had to get up and walk out of church. Man, my dad was so ticked off he didn't talk to me for a week. He was madder than a wet hen. But everybody knew it was old Willie. He was always doing crazy stuff like that. What made it so funny was that old Willie Blatz wasn't exactly the first thing that popped into your head if you were trying to think of the Lord. He was always leavin' farts. Willie, I mean."

"Did he get over it?"

"Willie?"

"No, your dad."

"After church, me and Willie apologized. But it was still funny when it happened."

"Did your dad forget it?"

"He still gets mad when I mention Willie Blatz's name."

"You and Willie were good friends?"

"Good friends?" Jim repeated. "You've got to be kidding! Man, we did everything together. I'm sorry you don't know Willie. Talk about somebody growing up and maturing! Man, he did it!"

"Was that sermon the only funny thing you remember?"

"Aw, no. What I just told you was kid stuff. But it was funny when it happened. Most everything I see strikes me funny. That's why that Ellen just about cracked me up. Life isn't funny because it's a joke. It's funny because it's so dumb. It doesn't make sense. My dad thinks everything in life is so serious."

"Maybe your dad has religious answers for everyday problems," Matt said.

"That's a mouthful. He's got an answer for everything. I sure don't."

"Don't what?" Matt asked.

"Have an answer for everything. Sometimes when I watch national news in the evening I don't think anybody has any answers. Just more questions and more problems."

"I don't catch the national news often. I'm outside working in the fields," Matt said.

"It's just as well you don't hear it," Jim said. "It's funny when people take everything so seriously like my dad. Don't get me wrong. Some things aren't funny at all. Like that old guy you were telling me about: the one who lost his sons in Korea. Old man Caffrey, you called him. I mean, for chrissake, there's nothing funny about that. But what sense does it make to raise three sons and lose every one of them because politicians want to fight some goddam war? Some things just aren't funny at all," Jim repeated. "Some things are so awful you have to laugh at little dumb things or else you'd go nuts. Does that make sense to you?"

Several moments passed without either speaking.

"Did his son ever come back from Canada?" Jim finally asked. "Mr. Caffrey's son?"

"No."

"Do they keep in touch?"

"Since Rob – that's his youngest – well, since Rob took off for Canada, old man Caffrey never mentioned his name again. Nobody in Willow Glen knows for sure whether they ever write or phone each other. It's like old man Caffrey never had a son called Rob. A couple years ago people around the Glen stopped asking about Rob 'cause whenever his name was mentioned old man Caffrey just turned his head and walked away."

Jim's eyes studied Matt's face carefully.

"Do you see Mr. Caffrey often?" Jim asked.

"Fourth of July and the County Fair."

"Don't you see him at church?"

"After Rob left for Canada, old man Caffrey stopped going. Nobody's seen him inside the church for a couple years."

Jim abruptly pointed to a field they were passing. "What do you call that stuff?" he asked.

"Soybeans."

"You ever work on a farm before?" Matt asked.

"Naw. My dad was pastor of a church in the inner city. The closest I ever got to a farm was watching movies and television."

"Think you can do the work?"

"If I don't do a good job, fire me."

"I always wondered," Jim went on, talking more to himself than Matt, "what it would be like working on a farm. Working outdoors all day long; doing work by myself. You know – if the job turns out good, you have only yourself to praise. And, if it doesn't, it's all your fault. I'll bet working on a farm is a lot like swimming. Just you against the elements. You don't have to depend on anybody else. That's good. Other people generally let you down. Well, not everybody. Willie Blatz, for instance. Man, I could always depend on him."

Matt pulled off the country road, onto the lane leading to his farmhouse. The western sky was filling with clouds. Not the kind that appear on a clear summer day, but those that precede rainshowers.

"Is this it?" Jim asked.

Matt didn't answer the obvious.

"What do you grow?"

"Corn. Wheat. And, a small vegetable garden."

"Any animals?"

"Few head of cattle."

Jim had both his hands on the car door where the window was rolled down and he was looking out like a child witnessing the family Christmas tree for the first time.

When the car stopped, Jim had the door open before Matt turned the ignition off.

"You don't even have to pay me! I'd work here for nothing," Jim shouted.

The offer sounded genuine.

"If I work here, what's my job?"

"I'll start you off easy," Matt said. "Tomorrow morning you can use the roto-tiller to cultivate the vegetable garden, then stake the tomato plants, then spray the apple trees, and finally cut the grass around the house. Then, in the afternoon...."

"You expect me to do all that in the morning?" Jim yelled.

Matt laughed as he walked toward the tractor still sitting beside the barn where he had parked it that morning.

With the suddenness that only a midsummer day can provide, the western sky suddenly spawned bluish-black clouds. In advance of these clouds the wind began chasing low-floating streaks of hazy clouds through the air while jagged webs of lightning crisscrossed the horizon.

"Better hurry, Jim. Before it starts to rain I want to show you how to run this tractor so you're used to it. Later in the week you can help bale the hay I cut in the pasture this morning."

The daylight sun was blocked by rolling clouds which made the late afternoon turn dusk-like. Wind was now gusting and small, light objects were hurtling through the air. The small American flag Greg attached to the handlebars of his tricycle became dislodged and as it blew through the air Matt jumped to catch the flag. He missed, but Jim ran after it and placed it in the tool box attached to the rear of the tractor.

"Jump up on the seat. I'll show you how to start this thing then you can drive it into the barn. It doesn't need any rain on it. It's got enough rust spots already."

Jim crawled onto the seat as Matt stood on the ground and gave directions on how to operate the piece of equipment. Matt's directions were clear and Jim was a quick learner. But they were not fast enough to beat the rain. The darkest clouds were still some distance from the farm, but large drops had already begun falling.

"Quick," Matt advised. "Drive it inside the barn."

Matt had no sooner spoken than the black clouds erupted with brilliant flashes of lightning followed by powerful claps of thunder. Jim drove the tractor inside the barn as Matt ran to the car to roll up the windows. When the tractor was inside, Matt hurried to close the barn doors behind the piece of equipment. It was now raining hard but the full force of the storm was yet some distance from the farm.

"Make a run for the house," Matt yelled. "Otherwise we'll be here till it stops raining."

They ran only a few feet beyond the barn when the full force of the storm hit. Suddenly the countryside turned dark. Rapid-fire bolts of thunder reverberated through the air, causing the ground to vibrate. Rain fell in torrents. By the time they reached the back porch of the house they were drenched.

"Whew!" Jim hollered. "Do storms always come up so fast around this part of the country?"

"Summer storms aren't unusual, but this one is worse than we usually get," Matt said.

Jim's hair was dripping and his rain-soaked clothes were clinging to his body. Puddles were already forming around his feet on the porch floor where water ran off his pants.

"If I have to put up with this weather, I don't know if I want to work here," Jim kidded.

"Here." Matt reached inside the kitchen door and grabbed a small washcloth that he offered Jim. The small cloth was useless in soaking up the water covering Jim.

Huddled against the back porch wall, they waited for some of the water to drain off their clothes. Jim cupped his hands around his right thigh and pushed his hands downward to force as much water as possible out of his pants. He did the same with his left leg.

The air appeared to be filled with phantom clouds which changed shape as they blew rapidly across the farmland, but looking closer, Jim realized it was the rain. Water was blowing across the land in sheets.

Not only was Jim's clothing soaked and uncomfortable; the quickly falling temperature made chills shiver across his flesh. He crossed his arms in a futile effort to ward off the sudden cold. And then he sneezed. Again. And yet a third time. Finally the discomfort was more than he could bear.

"You got a dryer in the house?" Jim asked.

"Right in the laundry room off the kitchen."

"Mind if I use it? Otherwise, I'll be here till midnight waiting for these clothes to dry out. Your wife won't mind, will she?"

"No... no, Marie won't care."

Matt walked to the screen door and held it for Jim to enter the house behind him. He led Jim through the kitchen and into the former walk-in pantry which had been converted to a small laundry room.

"Here." Matt pushed a knob on the dryer and pointed to a button. "When you've got your stuff inside, push this button and the thing will start."

Matt walked to the door of the small laundry room and turned to look at Jim again. Jim was still smiling as the water dripped from his hair onto this face and off his clothes onto the floor. Matt pulled the laundry room door closed behind him. He paused at the door.

Calling through the closed door, Matt said, "I'll be out in the bathroom changing into something dry myself."

Matt waited for an answer. There was none.

Matt walked to the bathroom. He pulled off his wet clothes, heavy with water. Once they were off, he grabbed a large bath towel and began rubbing it over his back and chest. The warmth of the towel felt good. He began to wipe the towel over his stomach and upper legs when he turned and saw Jim standing outside the open bathroom door.

"I put all my clothes in the dryer. Even my sneakers and shorts. But now I need a towel to dry off. Got one?" Jim smiled as he looked at Matt.

Matt's face flushed ever so slightly. It was so tanned that it was not noticeable to Jim, but Matt could feel the warm glow covering his face.

"Yeah, here's a towel.... Take it." Matt handed Jim a large bath towel from the top of the pile in the linen closet.

"Appreciate this," Jim said.

Matt resumed toweling the lower part of his legs.

"Wait a minute," Jim spoke up. "You missed a place here on your back."

With that, Jim grabbed the towel from Matt's hand and gently began rubbing it over the middle of Matt's back.

Matt stood motionless as the towel was rubbed over his back. When Jim was finished, Matt felt the warmth of Jim's body brush lightly against his back.

"There. That does it," Jim said as he handed the towel back to Matt.

"Hey, is this your ring?" Jim asked. He reached for the simple, gold wedding band that Matt had taken from his finger and placed next to the sink while he was drying off.

Before Matt could say anything, Jim slipped the ring on his finger.

"How about that? A perfect fit!" Jim said.

"Take that off," Matt ordered.

Jim didn't comment but quickly pulled the ring from his finger and replaced it on the counter as he looked at Matt.

Jim shrugged. "You're the boss." He slowly turned and walked toward the laundry room.

5

Storm damage was severe. Sections of the wheat field had been rain-whipped to the ground, and there was wind damage to the house and barn. Shingles had been blown away. Spouting fell off the front porch roof from the weight of the downpour. A few windowpanes in the barn were shattered by flying debris. And a large sugar maple near the front gate was uprooted.

Though the initial brunt of the storm had passed, the dark gray sky, unbroken by any promise of blue, warned of continuing rain. Claws of lightning that slashed through the clouds at the height of the storm had now withdrawn, but the sound of thunder continued to rumble like the roll of muffled drums.

"Sorry about the storm damage," Jim said, after he got into the car. It was the first time he spoke since Matt told him to take the ring off his finger.

"As if I didn't have enough to do already," Matt grumbled. "Now I have to take a couple extra days to make repairs."

"I'll be around to help," Jim said.

Neither spoke on the drive back to church. Words were not helpful. They could not reduce the time it would take to make repairs. And now, Matt's sole concern was with property damage.

Streams of water were draining riverward across the church parking lot in whose basin-like depressions miniature lakes were filling where the paving contractor had failed to plot drainage.

Sounds of talking and laughing could be heard above the constant splashing of rain on the trees as Matt and Jim jumped across the puddles of the parking lot to the church basement.

As they entered the basement door, the air within enveloped them like the clouds of a steamroom. The handrail above the steps felt sticky where varnish absorbed humidity. Even outdoors, the rain made everything feel gummy. But in the church basement where the crowd of people had gathered, the humid, stale-smelling air clung to the skin like clammy mist.

Walking down the steps, Matt eyed his wife and son. But it was not until he reached the bottom that Jim, who was behind him, said anything.

"Eight o'clock all right?" Jim asked.

"What?"

"Eight o'clock! Should I come to your place tomorrow morning at eight o'clock to start work?" Jim asked.

"Yeah. That's good. I'll be up long before then."

Jim disappeared into the crowd as a woman came toward Matt.

"Are you the one Jim's going to work for?"

The question was asked by a plump woman whose black hair was wound into a bun at the nape of her neck. Her general appearance and facial features might have belonged to hundreds of thousands of women; they were common in all respects, save one: her eyes. The sockets were deeply set; the lids, darkly colored. At first it looked like makeup – too much eye shadow; but a more careful examination revealed that the skin surrounding both eyes had assumed an unnaturally dark, almost bruised coloration. These eyes made their owner appear older than her years. And a contradiction masked her face: a ready smile greeted Matt, but the eyes betrayed the smile. Matt had become so preoccupied studying her eyes that it was not until she repeated her question that he answered.

"Is Jim going to work for you?" she asked again.

"Yes. Yes, he is," Matt answered. "Are you the preacher's wife? Mrs. Renalski?"

Since Matt knew everyone in the church basement, the question was less the result of guesswork than simple deduction.

"Why yes! Lord, how did you know? And with all these people! Everybody calls me Letty. My name's really Letitia. But that's so formal! Everybody calls me Letty."

That Matt recognized her visibly pleased Mrs. Renalski.

"My husband told me about Jim's work offer," she continued. "When will Jim start?"

"Tomorrow morning."

"That's good," the preacher's wife said. "That's very good. He needs something to fill his time. You know what they say about idle hands and the devil's workshop! When I went to high school I worked every summer. I wasn't paid for it, either. No sir. I worked at Bible camp. I was always busy. I think all young people should be kept busy, don't you? They have too much free time. And too much money. Really, too much of everything. That's why they watch so much television. And the kinds of awful programs they watch! Trash! Pure trash! That's what most of it is. It sends shivers up and down my spine when I think of some of the programs they show on some of these channels. Believe me, I've seen some advertisements! Men and women doing openly what decent people wouldn't even think about! Then the people who watch these shows go out and do what they see on the television. That's what's wrong with the world. Lord, I never had free time when I was young. Kids six years old know more today about the seamy side of life than I did when I got married. You know why? I went to Bible camp. I spent time working with needy youngsters. I did charity work when I was young. I still do. There were all sorts at the Bible camp. Colored kids from the ghetto. Foreign kids who just got off the boat. White kids from the slums. Hardly any were normal American kids. I think it's important to know how all sorts live, though, don't you? But when my husband had a chance to escape from the inner city to come to the country, Lord, I told him he'd better take it. Get away from all the trash that lives in the heart of a city. Praise the Lord, my prayers were answered. We got out here in the country with you farm folks. Where everything's clean and wholesome. Don't you think so?"

Letty's question tumbled out so suddenly after her monologue that Matt was caught off guard.

"Well... I guess that... I'll try to keep Jim busy," Matt stammered. "Jim looks like a good worker," he added.

"Good worker! You expect Jim to be a good worker?" she asked. "Maybe I shouldn't tell you, but he's never worked on a farm a day in his life. Lord, not one blessed day. You'll have to show him every single thing you want done. Every single thing. I'm not saying he can't do the work. But, I honestly don't know if he can or not. You may be disappointed. I hope not. But you may be. I tried to make him help out with Bible camp like I did when I was young. But do you think he'd do it? No sir, he would not. His father and I tried to talk to him, but would he listen? No. He did as he pleased. He needs discipline. Remember that! *Make* him do the work you give him. Sometimes I'm afraid for his soul. If he doesn't learn discipline I'm afraid it's lost. And with all the free time and television that young people have nowadays! I pray for his soul. I really do. Sometimes I'm afraid he's already lost. That's why I encouraged his father to come to this country parish. I hope you teach Jim discipline this summer. He needs it. He really does need it. He won't listen to anybody."

Matt's attention drifted away from the preacher's wife and over to the crowd. His eyes stopped when they came to Jim standing in a far corner of the room. Ellen had him cornered and his desperate grimace turned to a faint smile as he saw Matt speaking with his mother. Jim pointed to his mother and broke away from Ellen, who bared her braces at his departing form.

Scarcely stopping to catch her breath at her son's approach, the preacher's wife continued. "We were talking about you," she said. "I was telling Mr. . . . Mr. . . . what did you say your name is?"

"Justin," Matt replied. "Matt Justin."

"I was telling Mr. Justin that you've never worked on a farm and he'll have to show you everything he wants done. I told him to keep you busy, and I told him you need discipline. Do you think you'll be able to do the work for Mr. . . . Mr. . . . for this man?"

His mother's chatter only faintly reached Jim, whose gaze was fixed on Matt.

"If Jim doesn't really want to do the work," Matt said, glancing at Jim, "or if you need him to help around the church," Matt added, looking at Letty, "I can manage. I don't want to make anybody do work they aren't really interested in."

"Absolutely not!" Letty insisted. "I want Jim to work. And I want him to work on your farm. But remember: he needs discipline."

"I'm looking forward to it," Jim said finally. "Tomorrow morning, eight o'clock sharp. I'll be there."

Mrs. Renalski's words had given him some trepidations, but Matt was resigned to the situation. The matter was settled, for the present, and even if Matt had wished to squirm out of the deal with Jim, their conversation was interrupted when Greg spotted his father. Jim and Letty moved on as Greg came running.

"Look at my prize!" Greg shouted as he ran to his father. The boy proudly displayed the red balloon he had won in the children's games.

"He was the winner of the pre-schoolers' footrace," Marie explained, walking behind Greg.

"What does it say, Dad?" Greg pointed to the white-lettered words on the balloon.

"It says 'Keep America Strong.'"

Matt picked Greg up and held him in his left arm as they waited in line for their supper. Greg, tired from the day's excitement and in need of an afternoon nap, rested his head on Matt's shoulder and closed his eyes. His small fingers clutched the short string of the balloon.

"Did you make arrangements with the preacher's son to help with the work?" Marie asked Matt.

"It's all settled. He starts tomorrow. With the storm damage I'll need all the help I can get this week."

"Oh, no! What happened?" she asked.

"Torn shingles. Broken spouting. Windowpanes. The maple blew over. Nothing too major but there'll be plenty of fixing to be done."

"Well, that's just wonderful, isn't it?"

"It wasn't my fault," Matt shrugged.

"Now, I guess you'll never get around to painting the inside of the house," she said.

"Repairs should only take a couple days."

"Do you think that preacher's kid will be any help?" she asked.

"Seems willing. I hope so."

As Matt and Marie were speaking, the Reverend Renalski and his wife joined the buffet line immediately behind them.

"Gordan, with all these strange people milling around I'm feeling terribly faint," Letty whispered.

"Pull yourself together," the preacher ordered. "There's not one person in this room to be afraid of."

Letty closed her eyes and breathed deeply, then looked over the crowd.

"While everyone is here, will you announce our plans for the Bible camp?" she asked.

"This isn't the right time or the right place," he said.

"It's an ideal time and place to announce it. Everybody's here."

"I'll do it this Sunday. Bible camp should be announced at a formal service."

"You should do it this evening. Everybody's in a receptive mood."

"A picnic supper isn't the right time," the Reverend Renalski insisted.

"A picnic supper is the perfect time," she murmured.

"Their minds are on the picnic and the storm."

"The sooner it's announced, the sooner I'll get some help from the people."

"I'll help you."
"Like last year?"
"Yes."
"I did all the work myself last year."
"Several ladies at the church helped you."
"You didn't help."
"I was busy."
"Doing what?"
"Church work."
"Bible camp is church work."
"I was too busy for that."
"You spent too much time with that Loren Pritchind."
"I told you a million times that we had business that had to be attended to."
"I never did like that man," she said.
"He's got his head screwed on right. He knows what's going on. Good worker, too."
"I don't trust him. He's always got a scheme for something or other."
"You've just never taken the time to sit down and talk with him. He's got good ideas. And he's not afraid to stick his neck out."

Greg had fallen asleep on Matt's shoulder, but suddenly the child awoke and before Matt realized it, the child was pointing to Reverend Renalski's bald head and shouting, "Look, Daddy! No hair! No hair!"

Marie's cheeks turned bright red as she turned to the preacher.

"Children don't always say what their parents would like," she apologized.

Reverend Renalski ignored Marie's comment as he nervously passed his left hand over his bald pate. As the preacher returned his hand to his side his wedding band grazed the side of Greg's red balloon and the tissue-thin rubber burst with a loud pop.

Greg's mouth opened wide and he let out a piercing wail.

"Now, now," Letty cooed, "it's all right. I'll try to find another balloon for you." Looking at her husband, she added sharply, "It's not the first time my husband has burst someone's balloon," then hurried off.

Matt shifted Greg to his other shoulder and tried to distract him.

After they had passed through the cafeteria line and received their trays of food, Marie's father motioned them to the table at which he and the rest of her family were sitting.

"Did you pack a suitcase for yourself and Greg?" Marie's father asked as soon as they sat down.

"It's all packed," Marie said, "and in the back of Matt's car."

"Good," her father bellowed. "It'll be good to have you and Greg for a week. Sorry Matt can't join us, but I know the work won't wait."

Greg became preoccupied with his grandfather but it wasn't long before Letty returned, holding another balloon. This one was blue.

As late as that morning Matt had viewed Marie's vacation with casual indifference. He had hoped that some time away from each other would help their marriage, but her actual absence meant little to him. But now, after having met Jim and made arrangements with him to help on the farm, Matt awaited Marie's absence with pleasant anticipation. The change promised to be welcome even though the Renalski family posed as many questions as answers.

The red sky that had dawned that morning fulfilled its omen. The storm had not only drenched the countryside, but dampened the day's festivities as well. The traditional Fourth of July exercise precluded by the rain, most of the community was thrown into confusion. Rarely had their celebrations been disrupted in even the most trivial way, so to have a thunderstorm and continual rain – an act of God, everyone was calling it – was more than the village leaders were prepared for.

Every year, without exception, the ladies of the church prepared the picnic supper in the kitchen of the church basement. Then all the parishioners ate outside in the park shelter. But this year everyone was forced to eat supper in the moist and muggy basement.

And the fireworks! The ground was so wet that the fireworks display was out of the question, and the clouds gave no sign of clearing. It was one of those rare, midsummer rains that gave every indication of lasting long into the night. To have this one day of the summer so marred posed a problem that the village fathers could not resolve.

The annoyance Matt experienced upon seeing the damage to his house and barn gave way to mild amusement as he watched the people in the church basement. The irony of the situation did not impress him at first but the longer he watched the townsfolk the more entertained he became.

He looked in Jim's direction.

Ellen had planted herself on a chair beside Jim, talking nonstop, while Jim nodded inattentively.

Matt smiled at him.

Jim, in silent response, rolled his eyes.

6

At sunup next morning when Matt awoke his eyes remained closed as the last trace of dreams fled the drowsiness of waking. He turned his head on the pillow and looked to the window. Today the dawn was ordinary, the sky calm. Nothing like yesterday.

He swung his legs over the side of the bed and, hunching his elbows on his knees, he covered his face with his hands to capture a few more moments' rest. The house was quiet: no creaking floorboards, no other voices, only the steady rhythm of the clock.

Marie and Greg had left the picnic supper last evening with her father and now this morning Matt had the house to himself. There was a splendid freedom in walking across the floorboards without worrying whether it would awaken Marie or Greg. And after he dressed, when he went to the kitchen to prepare his breakfast, it made no difference if he rattled dishes or accidentally slammed the cupboard door because there was no one in the house to disturb.

He had hardly begun his cereal at the kitchen table when he got up, walked to the counter beside the kitchen sink, and turned on the small radio. Turning up the volume louder than usual, he listened to the newscaster complete the morning report. He waited for the weather forecast.

"After the heavy storms moved through the valley yesterday afternoon, the rain continued past midnight. But this morning the cloud cover has moved to the east and it should be a picture-perfect day. Humidity will be low. Temperature will be moderate. Not above seventy-five degrees. Sunshine will be with us all day. Our radar doesn't show any rain on the scope."

The forecast became fact during the early morning hours as Matt started his outdoor chores. He lost track of the time until he heard the sound of tires grinding into the gravel lane leading to the house. Stepping from inside the barn, he saw a late-model car slowing to a stop near the house.

Jim was out of the passenger side walking toward Matt before the car motor was turned off. Matt expected the car to be put in reverse but the driver's door opened and Letty got out.

"OK if I put this on the porch?" Jim waved a small plastic bottle of suntan lotion as he passed Matt.

"Sure."

"Where's the roto-tiller?" Jim hollered from the porch.

Matt pointed into the barn. "Be with you in a minute."

The preacher's wife began talking as she came toward Matt. All the while she let her eyes conduct a rapid inspection of the farm.

"Jim told me how to get here," she said. "My, isn't this the pretty place! A big barn. And a nice vegetable garden. I'll bet your wife freezes and cans all summer long. And all those open fields. But your house – it does need some paint. But I guess you're kept busy enough without painting. Some of the rooms inside the parsonage need paint, too. Dreadful! The colors on the wall right now are absolutely dreadful. Those dreary walls need paint. The living room walls are blue! Can you imagine that? Blue! Isn't that depressing? I really think that blue walls are depressing. Don't you? You and your wife and your little boy got away so fast last night I didn't get to see you. Is your wife in the house right now?"

Without waiting for an invitation, Letty started toward the back porch before Matt called after her.

"My wife's not here. She took Greg and they're spending a few days at her family's place."

"Oh!" The explanation brought a sudden look of surprise to Letty's face and a momentary pause to her chatter. She stood still, looked around the yard as though wondering what to do next, then squinted at Matt.

"Had she been there," Letty began, "I planned on chatting with her for a while... but since she's gone...."

Matt waited as she decided what to do.

"I'll visit some day when she *is* here," she decided emphatically.

Matt again waited.

Keeping her eyes on the barn, Letty continued in a lower voice: "Now you remember what I told you about my son. Keep him busy and make him do whatever work you give him...."

Her voice was suddenly drowned out by the roar of a motor coming from the barn. Jim was maneuvering the tiller through the barnyard toward the vegetable garden. The roto-tiller was not large and a five-horsepower motor would not have presented any difficulty to a seasoned gardener, but to one so inexperienced as Jim the equipment presented a challenge. His fingers clenched the handlebars so tightly that his arms vibrated out of control, the machinery pulling him, rather than he it, to the vegetable garden.

"Like to talk more," Matt yelled over the sound of the tiller, "but I'd better show Jim which rows to cultivate."

Smiling, he turned his back and walked away from the preacher's wife toward the garden. When he glanced back at the car, it was slowly turning in the driveway and heading toward the country road.

"This sucker's got a mind of its own," Jim yelled over the sound of the motor. "How do I control it?"

Matt reached down and pushed the metal off-switch until it made contact with the spark plug, turning off the motor.

"You won't be able to till anything until you knock the drag down."

"What do you mean? The drag?" Jim laughed.

"This thing." Matt kicked a horizontal V-shaped metal piece on the rear of the tiller. The lower side of the V fell to the ground.

"That metal rod digs into the ground," Matt explained, "and it forces the tines of the tiller into the ground. That way the drag does the work and all you do is guide it. Otherwise, your shoulders do all the work instead of the machine."

Matt pulled the cord to start the tiller again. "Here, I'll show you what I mean."

His chest pressed tightly against the younger man's back, Matt stood behind, Jim guiding his fingers on the handlebars until the tines were digging deeply into the soil.

"Got the idea now?" Matt called into Jim's ear.

Jim turned his head and nodded as Matt backed away.

The morning passed quickly and by lunchtime Jim had finished more chores than he expected. The heavy rains of the day before had fallen so quickly upon the parched earth that much of the water had drained off the vegetable garden immediately. As a result, the ground was not muddy and Jim tilled the garden with little difficulty. After the tiller pulverized the soil, the rows of vegetable plants looked taller. And the tomato plants, beaten to the ground by the wind and rain, stood twice as tall after Jim staked each of them. By noon he was already cutting the grass in the front yard around the house.

Lunchtime, for Matt, was less a time for conversation than for listening to the local grain quotations and market reports. It was a ritual Marie had learned to live with, and one which Matt impressed on Jim this first work day.

They ate in silence at the dinette set in the kitchen while the radio announcer recited in monotone the price of wheat, corn, beef, and hogs. Jim also learned of a new insecticide for half-runner beans and the art of pickling gherkins. The announcer brought the half-hour farm show to an end by reminding his listeners that a pond clinic would be held on Friday at the county agricultural station and that anyone with an excessive amount of pond algae would be interested in a new treatment being tested.

"I never thought anybody could talk for half an hour about weeds and dirt," Jim groaned.

"It's important. That's how I keep up with things."

Jim raised his eyebrows and rolled his eyes.

"I'm glad you showed me how to use that tiller this morning," Jim said. "I think I used it the right way but my shoulders are still sore. And that vibration. Man! Vroom, vroom, vroom!" Jim held out his arms and kept shaking them to show how he felt.

"I guess you get used to it after working outside," Jim said.

"I never notice it."

"Your muscles are used to it," Jim decided.

Matt didn't answer.

Jim was ready to leave the kitchen when he suddenly stopped at the kitchen door.

"I don't want to turn red as a lobster in this afternoon sun," Jim said, "so I brought along some suntan lotion. Mind smearing a little on my back?"

Without waiting for Matt's answer, Jim pulled his white T-shirt over his head. When he arrived at eight o'clock, the T-shirt had been pure white, but after working outside it had become smudged black with dirt and grease, and stained green from tomato leaves.

Matt watched as Jim returned from the porch with the suntan lotion. There was no mistaking the fact that Jim was no longer a boy. His build was muscular, his appearance mature. A wide strip of hair rose from the base of his stomach and thick hair covered his chest.

Matt, sitting at the kitchen table, kept his eyes fixed on Jim as he was handed the plastic bottle.

"How long you been married?" Jim asked.

He pulled up a dinette chair and straddled it with his back to Matt.

"Four years."

Matt took the cap off the plastic container and squeezed the bottle till the oily liquid oozed onto Jim's shoulder blades and down his back.

"Yesterday afternoon at the picnic I watched you and your wife. You didn't talk to each other very much," Jim said.

Matt didn't answer. Instead, he rubbed the lotion across Jim's shoulders and back.

"Put a lot on my upper back and shoulders," Jim directed. "That's where the sun really gets me."

"Don't you ever get out in the sun?" Matt asked. "Your skin's white as chicken feathers."

Jim turned his head to stare at Matt. "Chicken feathers?" Jim repeated. "For chrissake, that's the first time anybody told me I had skin that looked like chicken feathers! The first thing most people tell me is that I've got a hairy chest."

"Don't get huffy."

"When you're stuck in the inner city where the streets are lined with buildings over thirty stories high, you don't catch too many rays down on ground level. Know what I mean?"

Matt grunted.

"You're pretty good with your hand," Jim said, "You must rub your wife's back a lot."

"For a kid, you've got a big mouth," Matt shot back.

"I like to talk. Man, you're really tight-lipped. Don't you ever open up?"

For answer Matt continued to apply the suntan lotion. He swirled the oil over Jim's back till his flesh glistened.

"I didn't mean to pry or anything," Jim added. "Only trying to make conversation."

"Forget it," Matt said. "If a stranger can see it, it must be obvious to everybody. I mean about me and Marie."

Matt got up and stepped to the kitchen sink to wash his hands. Jim rose and reached for the plastic bottle to begin rubbing the oil over his arms and chest and stomach. When he finished he went to the kitchen sink and stood beside Matt.

"Before you get married, know what you're getting into," Matt advised.

Jim leaned against the cabinet next to the sink, his arms crossed. He studied Matt's face.

"Didn't you?"

Matt hadn't expected Jim to answer.

"Anyway," Jim continued, "who says I'm getting married?"

"I saw you and Ellen last night," Matt jabbed at him. "I think there's a special magic between you two." A smirk stole across Matt's face.

"Oh my God, there you go again. Man, she's like a leech. Did you see her beside me?"

"I saw it."

Jim screwed the cap back on the bottle of suntan lotion and with a sudden, boyish motion he punched Matt's arm playfully.

"You missed the best part though," Jim said. "After you and your wife and your kid left church, I was walking back to our house. Old Ellen comes along following right behind me. This is no lie, either. She walked right beside me and she was like an octopus in heat. No lie! Her hands were all over me. I didn't even say goodnight to her. I almost slammed the door in her face. It was the only way I could get rid of her. I'm not a prude or anything like that but I mean, after all, for chrissake."

"I'll bet you have to fight off all the girls," Matt laughed.

Jim's expression remained unchanged as he backed away from Matt.

"It's not the girls who interest me," Jim said. "Or the women, either."

He scanned Matt's face for a reaction.

"Oh?"

"Does it make any difference to you?" Jim asked. "I mean, do you mind? Should I have kept my mouth shut?"

"No." Matt's single word was spoken without emotion.

"Nobody else in Willow Glen knows," Jim explained. "If you don't mind, I'd like to keep it that way. I'll be leaving for college in September."

"Not even your parents?" Matt questioned.

"I said nobody. And nobody means nobody, doesn't it?" Jim's voice had the slightest edge of agitation.

Matt's eyes never looked at Jim as he continued washing the dishes and putting them into the cupboard.

"I guess I just wanted you to know," Jim said. "Maybe I should've kept my mouth shut."

Matt didn't answer.

Neither said anything as they left the kitchen and went outside to begin their afternoon work.

As they walked back toward the vegetable garden, Jim stopped short. "Don't you have anything to say?"

Matt paused and looked back at Jim. "While I'm getting some new shingles for the barn, you can continue cutting the grass around the house."

Jim shook his head and muttered something under his breath that Matt couldn't hear.

While Jim finished cutting the grass, Matt drove to the Building and Farm Supply Store to buy replacement shingles for those ripped from the roof by the storm. Encountering no delays that afternoon, Matt accomplished even more work than he had planned. By late afternoon, repairs on the house and barn roof were almost completed. Throughout the afternoon his conversation with Jim dealt only with their work. Not until the ladders had been returned to the barn was anything more said.

"You can use the phone whenever you want," Matt said, "to have your mom or dad come after you... or, if you want, I can drive you home."

"Impossible," Jim said.

Matt turned, without speaking, to look at Jim.

"What do you mean?" Matt asked. "Impossible?"

"It's impossible for my mom or dad to come till late this evening. I didn't want to say anything this morning, but...."

Jim hesitated, as though waiting for Matt to say something.

"I told my parents that you said I could stay here overnight... I'll sleep in the barn... if you don't mind... you don't mind, do you?"

"I never told you that," Matt complained. "There was nothing in our deal about you staying overnight. Even if you do, you're either going to get dead tired or bored stiff 'cause my workday doesn't stop till sundown. And that means we'll be working till nine this evening. It's only about four now."

"That's all right," Jim insisted.

"That gripes me. It really does," Matt grumbled. "I never told you to stay."

"No problem. I'll keep working as long as you like," Jim said.

"We won't eat till we stop working tonight," Matt threatened.

"I'd rather be working here than doing nothing at home."

Matt accepted the inevitable; Jim wanted to stay. Matt gave in.

By nine o'clock the sun had settled below the horizon but the countryside was still cradled in the warm glow of dusk. The sounds of machinery stilled, only the rustling of leaves stirred the silence as the evening breeze blew across the twilit fields.

Matt and Jim, finished for the day, walked toward the back porch of the house. The oil that had glistened on Jim's back and chest at noon had all but disappeared, mingled with the sweat and dust of his labor. Though a steady worker, Jim was not accustomed to the effort required to work in the sun all day.

"Supper won't be much," Matt said. "But if you want to get cleaned up before eating, you'll feel better."

Jim didn't say anything as he trudged into the bathroom. By the time he had cleaned up, Matt had made some hamburgers and warmed some canned vegetables.

Jim appeared in the kitchen doorway in a pair of Matt's Levi's and wearing one of Matt's clean white T-shirts.

"Hope you don't object," Jim said. "I found these in the bathroom. I put my own clothes in the washer. I'll put mine back on as soon as they're out of the dryer."

Jim slumped in a chair at the kitchen table and slid down until the back of his head was on a level with the chairback. He closed his eyes and crossed his arms as Matt brought the dishes of food to the table.

"Your mother should be happy," Matt said. "She told me to make you work hard. 'Discipline is what he needs. Discipline.'"

They both laughed.

"The way I feel now, she'd be deliriously satisfied." Jim let his arms drop to his side but kept his eyes closed as Matt began eating supper.

"She's quite a talker," Matt said.

"She doesn't mean any harm."

"Does she always bombard a person with so many questions?"

"Yes."

"It would drive me crazy," Matt said.

"You get used to it. I ignore it."

"You can't even answer her. She talks too fast."

"She's got her reasons. Someday I'll tell you about it," Jim said, sitting upright. Conversation was suspended as he attacked his plate.

"Hey, not bad!" Jim said. "You're a good short-order cook."

"For a preacher's son you're not at all what I expected," Matt said. "Fact is, you're totally different than I thought you'd be."

"Disappointed?"

"I don't know how to treat you."

"Why don't you try treating me the same as you'd treat anybody else?"

At that, the first bites of food on an empty stomach made a long, rumbling belch come from Jim.

"Ooops! Excuse me," Jim muttered.

"Things like that!" Matt explained.

"You too?"

"What do you mean?" Matt countered.

"Because of my dad's work everybody thinks they've got me all figured out before I even say anything. For a change I wish people would stereotype the kids of insurance salesmen, or the kids of tuna fishermen, or the kids of pretzel bakers."

Without prodding, Jim continued: "When I was in grade school I tried to live up to everybody's idea of what a preacher's son should be. But then I got in high school. I realized I have my own life. And I found that I'm different...."

After they finished supper, Jim cleared the table without being asked. He began washing dishes before Matt finished the last food on his plate.

"I'm too tired to do anything except sleep," Jim said. "I'll just head out to the barn."

Jim glanced at Matt.

Matt's left eyebrow rose. "You don't have to sleep in the barn. Follow me."

A quick laugh escaped from Jim.

Matt walked from the kitchen through the small hallway to the bedrooms. He stopped at the bedroom door where Marie and Greg usually slept and flipped on the switch for the ceiling light.

Matt stalled at the doorway but Jim moved past him and went directly to the bureau on top of which was sitting a family portrait of Matt, Marie, and Greg. Jim picked it up and studied it.

"Recent photo?" he asked. "Looks new."

"Taken last Christmas. See the tree? In the background?"

"H'm," Jim acknowledged.

"That's when we got Greg his tricycle."

"Oh."

"Marie's wearing my Christmas gift to her. See that pin on her dress. She went crazy when she saw it in a catalogue, so I sent away for it. I thought it would make her happy."

"Did it?"

Matt shrugged.

"Greg's a cute kid," Jim said. "Smart, too. But I hope you don't expect me to twist up into a pretzel and sleep in this little bed of his. Do you want me to sack out over here?" Jim motioned to Marie's bed.

"Uh... there's a big double bed in my bedroom," Matt offered.

Tired as he was, Jim was not slow.

"What do you mean – your bedroom?"

"Uh... Marie stays with Greg through the night. In case he gets sick. Or has a nightmare. Any kind of emergency can come up when you've got a kid Greg's age."

"If you say so," Jim said.

Jim asked no more questions and made no other comments as he walked past Marie's bedroom into Matt's. He turned, waiting for Matt to follow.

"I won't be to bed for a while. Got some government farm reports to make out first," Matt explained.

"Are you sure that's the reason?"

"What other reason would there be?"

Jim pulled the clean white T-shirt over his head.

"Which side is yours?" Jim asked, looking at the bed.

Matt pointed to the window side.

"I'll lay still through the night so I won't wake you," Jim offered.

Matt's gaze rested less on Jim than on the room itself, his eyes roving around the room.

"Did you hear me?" Jim asked. "I said I won't bother you through the night."

"Yeah, yeah.... I'll get the reports finished," Matt answered distractedly as he left the room.

It was a few minutes after eleven before Matt finally finished his paperwork and turned off the light above the kitchen table.

Quiet though he was Matt's footsteps caused the wooden floors to creak loudly. After Matt had undressed in the darkened bedroom and eased himself into the bed, the bedsprings whined shrilly.

"Is there anything in this house that doesn't creak, rattle or squeak?" Jim asked as he began to laugh. Jim's reaction broke the tension.

"You mean the springs?" Matt asked, breaking into a chuckle. "It's been a while since I've had a good laugh over anything in this room."

"I can believe that. It's too bad your wife isn't twenty years older."

"How's that?"

"She'd make a good match for my father. They'd probably both get a kick out of going to funerals."

"You're nuts."

Matt laughed again.

"I mean it!" Jim said. "When I saw the two at the picnic yesterday, all I could think about was two Puritans, all happy and contented, on their way to a public hanging. How old is Marie?"

"Twenty-two," said Matt.

"My dad's got underwear older than that."

"Goodnight," Matt said.

"I guess that's the signal for me to shut up."

"Goodnight," Matt repeated.

"I get the message."

They both remained motionless, each on his opposite corner of the bed, a wide space between them. They lay some time before speaking again. Jim stirred.

"You asleep yet?"

"No."

"Can I say something without you punching me out?"

"I guess so. What is it?"

Jim paused.

"Well," Matt said, "are you going to tell me or not?"

Another pause.

Jim cleared his throat before speaking. "I love you," he said finally.

Matt said nothing.

On his side of the bed Jim was too far away to feel Matt's heartbeat quicken.

Another long pause followed before Jim spoke again.

"I mean it," Jim insisted. "I love you."

Silence filled the room.

Matt listened as the sighs of Jim's heavy, drowsy breathing fell, deeper and further apart, into sleep.

Matt, however, lay between sleep and wakefulness, where reality blurred but dreams shone clear. That very clarity caused him to awaken with a start from each successive dream, only to close his eyes once more, to dream again. His mind turned to Marie and Greg. Their first day of vacation was gone. Marie had so looked forward to it. And Greg always enjoyed going away, especially to his grandfather's farm. When they returned, perhaps he and Marie could make a fresh start. They were still young and not yet so set in their ways that change was impossible. They could make adjustments, learn to solve their problems together. Perhaps they could become closer than they had been in recent years. Perhaps the routine and apathy of their marriage could serve as a new starting point. It had been so long since he had kissed Marie; even longer since she had lain beside him in this bed.

Jim turned from his side onto his back. The gentle rocking of the mattress caused Matt to awaken but Jim still snored softly.

In his dreams, Matt was always confident of the success of his marriage. But now that he was awake the futility of his hopes pressed upon him with bitter derision. It was a dream he had had so many times before but, obstinately, the dream never became reality. And the depression upon waking tightened ever more firmly; it was like a vise slowly squeezing life from his body and hope from his spirit.

Matt stared into the bedroom darkness as Jim turned, facing him. Instead of moving away, Matt gently moved his arm until it encircled Jim's shoulder and back. In turn, Jim inched his body closer to Matt's until the warmth of their chests and faces touched. After a long, caressing embrace, each released his grasp of the other.

Matt's words were whispered softly, but they were all Jim needed to hear.

"I love you, too," Matt said.

7

The congregational singing of "Onward Christian Soldiers" carried through the valley the following Sunday morning as the worship service neared completion, and whether it was due to a final burst of religious fervor or anticipated dismissal from the stuffy church, the recessional hymn was sung more enthusiastically than the processional song had been.

The choir sat behind the communion table and from their tiered seats the singers appeared to roost in a giant crow's-nest from which a vigilant eye might be kept on each member of the congregation. From his perch, Jim watched Matt with rapt attention. Ellen sat in the choir immediately beside Jim and her face shone with a beatific satisfaction. She held her hymnal high not only so Jim could see the music with ease, but also so that she could watch him as he sang.

It was at Jim's urging that Matt attended the service but after he arrived at church he did feel like a hypocrite. If his presence at the service was inspired by the call of the Lord, Jim was certainly the messenger. It was the first time in many months that Matt had attended a service.

Marie, who joined her husband before the service began, looked rested. The week's vacation had worked its recuperative powers well on her and when she approached the sanctuary for communion there was new bounce in her step.

Once the recessional was finished, the members of the congregation crowded into the aisle to leave the church but the preacher, greeting each parishioner with a personal word at the door, prevented anyone's quick exit.

"You've certainly kept Jim busy this past week," the Reverend

Renalski said to Matt. "Apart from the time or two you brought him to the parsonage for clothing, we've hardly seen him."

"I appreciated the help," Matt admitted. "Got a lot of work done."

"No, no," the preacher insisted. "It's my wife and I who are appreciative. We're glad to see Jim kept busy. That's what he needs. Hard work. Discipline. You're just the tonic Jim needs."

Matt smiled at that.

The preacher's wife stood to the side and listened while her husband spoke. Again, her smile seemed to mask another expression, but it was impossible to tell what lay hidden beyond those wide, hurt eyes.

Marie, Greg, and Matt took their leave but had walked only a few steps when Letty ran up behind them.

"I really don't like to bother you," Letty interrupted, "but I have a big favor to ask."

"Oh?" Matt pursued more out of politeness than interest.

"Really, I need the favor from the missus," she added. "I need someone to help with the Bible camp this summer and I wonder if you'd be so kind? The first week of July is already gone and we want to have the camp in August and I don't know what I'll do if I don't get some help. There's registration and lesson plans and preparing lunches and transportation and artwork and I don't know how many other odds and ends connected with it. I've already told you I can't depend on Jim to help out. I told you he won't turn a hand for Bible camp. I've asked in the past but he won't help. Remember? And then there's all the regular work to be done around the parsonage. Now, you tell me, how do I do all the regular work in addition to preparing Bible camp? I've only got two arms, two legs, and twenty-four hours a day. I can't do the impossible. I know Gordan thinks I can, but I can't. And Gordan has his own work to do. Really, I need the help. And on top of everything else, I don't even think I'll have time to paint those living room walls till September. I'll be forced to live with those dreadful blue walls till Bible camp is finished. That's why I need your help. Do you think you have the time?"

Marie glanced at Matt.

He shrugged.

"Whatever you want." Matt's tone encouraged Marie to follow her preference.

"If you say no, I don't know what I'll do. I must have some help," the preacher's wife insisted.

Marie again looked at Matt. Again, shrugging his shoulders and raising his eyebrows, he passed the responsibility for the decision onto his wife.

"Well, I guess it would be a good way to keep me and Greg busy next month," Marie admitted.

The preacher's wife clasped her hands together and raised her eyes skyward. "Praise the Lord, that's settled," she said.

Jim came running from the side door of the church and he called to Matt.

"Want me to start work tomorrow morning about eight?"

"Between then and nine," Matt answered.

When Marie saw Jim she began walking with Greg and Letty to their '68 Chevy in the parking lot.

"Won't have to worry about my getting back and forth to your farm anymore," Jim exclaimed. "I got myself a set of wheels."

"You got a car?" Matt asked incredulously.

"Naw, not a car. Where would I get that kind of money?"

"What then?"

"A bike."

"You mean a motorcycle?" Matt asked.

"Yeah. It's kinda beat up, but it'll get me around Willow Glen," Jim said. "Last week we talked so much about Mr. Caffrey that yesterday afternoon after I left your place I got curious so I found out from the church records where he lived and I just drove my dad's car out to his farm. We had a nice long talk. He's a nice guy."

"You didn't say anything to him about his sons, did you? I mean, about the two killed in Korea or the one in Canada? That gets him upset."

"My gosh no. How dumb do you think I am? We just talked. I told him all about working at your place. Being a minister's kid. Stuff like that."

"You didn't tell him about... about you and me, did you?" Matt asked.

"You mean that we're lovers?"

"Ssshhh!" Matt's eyes darted around to see if anyone was close. There was no one.

"For chrissake, no," Jim said. "Me and old man Caffrey just had a nice talk. That's all. Then when I was ready to leave, all of a sudden he asked me if I have my own car. I told him no and that's when he took me back to his barn and wheeled out this bike. He told me I could have it if I wanted it – that he didn't have any use for it anymore. He said it belonged to Rob."

"Did he charge you for it?"

"Not a dime. He said he was only happy if somebody my age could get some use out of it. He said Rob wouldn't be using it anymore."

"Don't tell me that's how you'll get to my farm from now on?" Matt asked.

"Sure. Why not? It'll be a good way to get around."

Matt turned so only Jim could hear. "I'm really sorry you won't be able to stay all night now that Marie's home."

"That's life," Jim said. "We'll still be able to get together. There'll be plenty of times for that." Then, speaking a bit more loudly, Jim added, "This bike will give me transportation back and forth to your place, anyway."

Matt smiled as he raised his arm in a wave to Jim and began walking to his '68 Chevy in the parking lot.

The brief encounter with Mrs. Renalski and Jim established the schedule for July and August. Marie, intent on doing a good job at the Bible camp, spent her mornings and afternoons with Greg at the country church; only her evenings and nights were spent in the farmhouse with Matt. Her new interest left little time to worry about her husband.

Matt, in turn, accomplished more work on the farm than he had done for a long time. Repairing fences, painting the barn, general upkeep: for the first time in years, he was gradually getting on top of his work.

And then there was Jim, without whom the farm work would still be accumulating. He came every morning, worked all day, and left late in the afternoon. Matt and Jim spent their workdays together.

The daily schedule became routine.

Matt's life with Marie, however, remained unchanged. Matt slept in his room, Marie in hers. Their only mutual concern was Greg. The reconciliation Matt had dreamed of remained a dream.

On the twentieth of August Marie was up early preparing cutouts on colored construction paper to take to Bible camp. Though she had worked late the night before, her lesson plan lay unfinished so she rose early to complete her work.

She had packed all her material into a shopping bag near the kitchen door and placed her lesson plans for Bible class in a manila folder on the kitchen table when Matt called from his bedroom.

"I'm going to the Farm Supply Store today. Need anything?"

She walked through the hallway to his bedroom with the manila folder in her hand.

"If it's no trouble I need more writing paper. You can pick up three or four large boxes of crayons, too. The kids are always breaking or losing what they have at camp."

Marie stopped in his doorway and watched as he measured the walls of the bedroom.

"What are you doing?" she asked in surprise.

"Measuring for paint."

"I didn't think you'd remember."

"I told you I'd get to it."

"Will you paint every room?"

"Probably only the bedrooms now. I'll do the other rooms later. Maybe September."

Marie's eye was drawn to the paint charts on the bureau and she stepped into the room to examine the color chips. Picking up the charts with one hand, she laid down her manila folder with the other.

"I like this oyster white," she said. "It'll go with anything. If it's in stock I'd like that in my bedroom."

"No problem. One color's as easy to put on as another."

"Now don't get the most expensive paint," she suggested. "But something that can be washed."

"What color are you putting on your walls?" she asked.

He shrugged. "Any ideas?"

"If you want to match the bedspread, why don't you get this light green... or maybe a pale yellow... no... light green would be better. This one – Spring Mist." She pointed to the chip.

"I may not get your room finished in one day," Matt said.

Marie stuck her tongue between her teeth and wrinkled her nose.

"Well, I guess for one night I can fix a place for me and Greg out in the living room," she said.

"You could sleep in here."

He watched her face.

She glanced around the room and her eyes settled on the bed.

"It won't be any trouble fixing a place in the living room," she answered.

With that, she turned to walk down the hallway.

After several moments Marie called from the kitchen door. "I'm leaving now. Greg's already out in the car."

Matt grunted a goodbye.

He was measuring the walls as he heard the car motor start. He listened as it pulled away from behind the house. The sound of tires crunching over gravel grew faint as the Chevy coasted down the driveway to the road. After all sound had faded into silence, he began writing the dimensions of the walls on a piece of paper, subtracted the square footage for door and window openings, and determined how many gallons of paint he needed for the two bedrooms.

A shadow, flickering against the bedroom wall, followed by the low hum of a motor, caused Matt to glance up. Matt watched Jim get off his motorcycle in the backyard and he continued to watch as Jim passed the window.

Jim saw Matt inside the room and waved.

His work outdoors had turned Jim's complexion from pale pink to ruddy tan. After several days on the farm he stopped wearing the long Levi's that sheathed his legs and began wearing cut-offs. Thick hair that covered his legs remained dark; too dark to become sun-bleached. His leg muscles were strengthened through the daily chores and his skimpy cut-offs revealed powerful thighs. Working on the farm turned his late adolescent swimmer's frame into well-defined muscle.

During the past six weeks Jim had come to view Matt's farm as a second home. He had the run of the farm and the run of the house. After the first days he knew which chores had to be done and he did them without being asked. He knew what had to be repaired and he did the work without prodding. He was less a helper than someone with a vested interest in the property. He had ceased being a hired hand many weeks ago. Jim had become Matt's spouse.

The kitchen screen door slammed and footsteps approached Matt's bedroom.

"What's new?" Jim asked, propping himself in the doorway, leaning against its frame.

"Measuring the walls," Matt explained.

"What for?"

"To buy paint."

"I thought you weren't painting till October."

"Changed my mind... so you can help," Matt said.

Matt playfully jabbed Jim above the elbow with his fist.

"OK, if that's what you want...." Jim didn't finish the sentence but spun around and lunged toward Matt. Jim grabbed him from behind the waist.

Matt laughed as he tried to break loose from Jim's grip. "So you want to fight, huh?"

Jim pinned Matt's arms behind him. Suddenly Matt broke loose, turned around, and flung himself against Jim so quickly that Jim was pushed backward and fell onto the bed. Not expecting Jim to fall backward, Matt plunged forward and landed on top of him.

Both laughed and, winded from the sudden exertion, they stopped their horseplay. Matt waited to catch his breath, and in the slight pause that followed, he suddenly felt Jim's face rise, and Jim's lips were touching his. Matt did not resist when the warmth of Jim's tongue pressed against his own. Only after several moments did Matt lift his face from Jim's.

Matt got up and stepped away from the bed. He turned his back and quickly stepped to the window. But Jim made no effort to get up. Instead he swung around in bed until his head rested on the pillow. He stretched out on the bed.

Several moments passed but the only sound was an occasional creaking of floorboards as Matt shifted his feet to stare out the window.

"What's the matter? You mad?" Jim finally asked.

"I've got a wife. And a son."

"So? What's the difference?"

"So, I'm married," Matt said in a louder voice.

"Really?"

The single word was blade-sharp.

Matt neither answered nor moved from the window.

"Jim, I'm getting worried. In only a couple weeks you'll be leaving Willow Glen for college. I don't know if I can take that."

Matt turned his head from the window to Jim, lying on the bed. The look was long.

Jim responded by slowly sitting upright, then getting out of bed. When he came to stand behind Matt at the window, the front of his T-shirt pressed against Matt's back as they stared out the bedroom window.

"Ever since we met last month we've been lovers," Jim said quietly. "Why don't you leave Marie? We can live together. I'll go to school. Maybe find a part-time job. You can work. We don't have to leave each other."

"I'm married."

"You admitted there's nothing between you and Marie."

"There's Greg."

"Are you staying with Marie only for Greg? How much longer can that go on?"

"This is Willow Glen, not some big city."

Jim continued standing behind Matt and when he slowly clasped his fingers around Matt's hand, Matt did not push him away.

"I can't do anything to hurt Marie. Or Greg," Matt said.

"Is Marie happy with your marriage now?"

"Things will improve. We need time, that's all."

"Always hoping that tomorrow will be better!"

"What do you mean?" Matt asked.

"Can't you see it? Your marriage is dead. And you're dying too. So is Marie. Not physically, but emotionally."

"That's not true. Things will get better."

"You're a dreamer, Matt. All you've got in life is today. This hour. This minute. You're always dreaming about how things will get better in the future. You've got to make your life what you want it to be."

"You're the dreamer," Matt said. "Always looking for simple answers to complex problems."

"I'm honest," Jim said.

"You've got to plan. You've got your whole life to live. Set goals. Make something of it."

"Man, where have I heard that sermon before?" Jim said. "Mr. Caffrey's sons had their lives. They were young too."

Jim rested his head against Matt's.

"Before you came here I only had one worry. My marriage."

"Are you saying you've got another worry now?" Jim asked.

"You want to hear it from me?" Matt asked. "All right, I'll tell you. I feel about you the way I always thought I should feel about Marie. And I feel guilty about it. It goes against everything I was always taught. Now, are you satisfied?"

"You think I caused that?" Jim asked.

"If you'd never come to Willow Glen, I'd have only my first worry. My marriage."

"If it hadn't been me," Jim answered, "it would've been some other man. Some day. Some man. Some way. You would have found out about yourself."

"Wouldn't you know it?" Marie complained as soon as she stepped into the parsonage.

"Now what's the matter?" Letty asked.

"My lesson plans. They're home. In a manila folder on the bureau in the bedroom. I looked at some paint charts and I laid the folder down and drove off without it."

"Can't you get through the day without your lesson plans?"

"Not after all the work I spent on them last night and this morning! I got up early this morning just to finish the work. It won't take more than twenty minutes to go home after them."

Parents were dropping off their children in the church parking lot as Marie got into the '68 Chevy and headed back home.

As she pulled into the driveway to the farmhouse there was no one in sight. She was in such a hurry that she stopped beside the front door, jumped out of the car, and was searching through her key ring as she stepped onto the front porch.

The key slid into the lock easily and she left the front door ajar as she hurried through the living room toward the hallway and the bedrooms. The instant she reached the hallway she stopped. She heard Matt.

She walked more slowly.

Her footsteps became more deliberate.

Then she reached the doorway and looked into the bedroom.

Jim and Matt were together naked on the bed, their bodies clasped together in sexual union, as they groaned with pleasure.

She stared.

Matt did not see Marie. Nor did Jim.

She made a move and Jim saw her.

Then Matt glanced upward toward the door and saw his wife.

She slowly walked to the bureau and picked up the manila folder.

Once at the bedroom door, she stopped and turned.

Her words were calm, resigned, final.

"Matt... our marriage is over."

8

Matt and Jim, lost in thought, spent the morning in the kitchen: Jim alternately rested his head in his arms on the tabletop or sat upright on the dinette chair, while Matt poured himself cup after cup of hot coffee. He cleared his throat repeatedly but said nothing.

It was sometime before noon when the sound of tires grinding over pebbles came from the driveway. The rumbling of the engine slowed, then stopped. The dull thud of a car door slamming was followed seconds later by a persistent knocking at the back door.

Matt got up and went to the screen.

"I think we should talk." The Reverend Gordan Renalski stood outside, squinting his eyes as he spoke through the screen door.

The preacher's dark gray suit, white collar, and black rabat made his appearance more stark than usual. His face glazed into a rigid stare as he peered through the screen.

Matt opened the door.

"I won't waste words. Marie told me what she saw this morning," Reverend Renalski said. "She's terribly upset. Distraught. It's obvious there's nothing to discuss. I've simply come after my son. I thought he'd be home by now."

The preacher directed his comments to Matt and ignored his son.

Jim folded his arms against his chest. His shoulders pressed against the back of the kitchen chair on which he was sitting.

"Jim." His son's name, spoken by the minister, was less a term of address than a command.

Jim's eyes darted to Matt.

"Maybe Jim doesn't feel like going with you. He's got work to do here this afternoon," Matt said.

"His work here is finished. Forever."

"Why don't we let Jim decide that," Matt said.

Matt tried to speak with force and conviction but he persistently cleared his throat and frequently raised his right hand to his mouth.

"Face facts, Mr. Justin. Several other ladies at the church this morning overheard your wife. They didn't hear much, but rumors will start. Your reputation is already damaged in the community. It will get worse. Much worse. You're not going to ruin my son's reputation. It's quite clear to me that you forced him into this situation."

The tip of Matt's tongue encircled the inside of his lips in vain effort to moisten his mouth for speech.

"Let me explain the facts to you, Mr. Justin. You see, you're a married man. You have a three-year-old son. My own son is a boy recently graduated from high school. Although he is legally of age, he is still my boy. You've taken advantage of his youth, and quite simply, I've come to take him out of this environment."

Reverend Gordan Renalski said nothing as he moved to the screen door. He paused and turned to look at Jim.

"You must return home with me. Now. And never come back here," the preacher said to his son.

"So, your son likes men rather than women," Matt spoke up. "What's so terrible about that?"

The preacher took a deep breath and stared at Matt.

"What's so terrible about that, you ask? Let me explain some things to you," the preacher began. "I'll be honest with you, Mr. Justin. Homosexuals are less than men. They're weak. They cast a shadow on those of us who are real men. I've seen those homosexuals in the bigger cities. And I resent them more every time I see them. They won't take on the responsibility of raising a family. They want their heaven right here on earth – sexual pleasure, no responsibilities, carefree life, money to burn. They're evil. Corrupt. Their lifestyle is decadent. They have far too many good things here on earth. That's why I've worked so hard in opposing gay rights in every city where I've ministered. Homosexuals shouldn't merely go to hell after death. They should also suffer hell on earth. Homosexuals need to be punished. Maybe if they can't find employment or housing they'll learn how difficult life is for those of us who live like men should live. Fortunately I have a job in which I can influence other people. And believe me, I'd do all in my power to prevent any queer from ever gaining any legal rights."

"And what if two homosexuals really love each other? Like me and

Jim. Shouldn't we have that right to love each other?" Matt pressed.

"Homosexuals are not the least bit different than rapists. Rapists aren't real men. They're cowards who attack and viciously assault women. They don't have sex. They enjoy violence. And homosexuals are the same. They don't love each other. They attack each other and use sex as a form of violence."

"That's not the way it is at all," Matt protested.

"Save your breath, Matt. He won't listen," Jim said quietly.

By the time the preacher had finished speaking, his face was blanched. The opportunity to speak his mind seemed to give him a particular satisfaction.

Jim looked at his father. The preacher's chest heaved slightly with each breath and his face remained expressionless as he looked at his son. The preacher held the screen door open but Jim remained seated at the dinette table. The eyes of father and son met.

"I know what you did to Mom. But you're not going to do it to me." Nothing softened the look of determination on Jim's face.

The preacher waited a moment before closing the door and leaving the porch. After he was gone, Matt sat across from Jim at the kitchen table.

"Now what?" Matt asked.

"Maybe it's time for me to get out on my own," Jim said. "Probably shouldn't have moved here to Willow Glen in the first place."

"Where will you go?"

Jim shrugged.

"Even if you do as your father wants and return home, I don't think I'll feel any different toward Marie," Matt said.

Jim raised his eyebrows and shrugged again.

"But I can't just walk out on Marie. Or Greg. I'd miss him more than Marie."

"Can you imagine what'll happen when word gets around? This is a small town. A real small town. Rumors. Gossip. What's your life going be like?" Jim's questions drew Matt's forehead into a worried pucker.

"Maybe," Matt began, "I could get away for only a couple days. Think things out. It all happened so fast. Too fast. Can't decide what to do now. But if your father starts shooting off his mouth about my...." Matt stopped in mid-sentence. "And you heard him say that, didn't you? That's really great; just what I needed."

Matt went to the stove and poured himself another cup of coffee. For some time he said nothing.

"Do you want to come with me?" Matt finally asked Jim.

"Are you leaving Marie?"

"Maybe. I don't know. Probably not."

"Leaving Willow Glen?"

"Maybe."

"Where to?"

"I don't know. Just away from here."

"How long?"

"What do you mean?" Matt asked.

"How long do you plan on staying away? Till midnight? Tomorrow morning? Next week? How long?"

"I don't know."

"Oh, for chrissake. Don't you know anything?"

"Well, how am I supposed to know?"

Matt raised the coffee cup to his mouth and drained it.

"When you leaving?" Jim asked.

"Right now," Matt said.

"How're you leaving? On your tractor?" Jim asked sarcastically.

Matt raised his hand to his head and rubbed his fingers through his hair.

"I'll get my car from the church. Maybe I can hitch a ride there. Marie and Greg will get home some way. One of the other ladies can bring them back. After I get my car, I'll come back here. Pick up some clothes and get out of here for a day or two. Maybe longer. I don't know."

"Are you sure that's what you want to do?" Jim asked skeptically.

Matt didn't answer at first.

"You coming with me?" Matt finally asked.

Jim rolled his eyes and sighed heavily as he turned to look down the hallway to Matt's bedroom.

"Jesus Christ, Matt. I don't know. To pick up all of a sudden and leave here for God-only-knows-where. I don't know, Matt. I mean, after all, for chrissake. This isn't exactly the way I always planned on leaving home and going out on my own. This isn't the way I expected things to turn out at all."

Matt's eyes revealed neither encouragement nor disgust nor anger nor love. Their neutral expression was the same inscrutable gaze Marie had long ago given up trying to understand.

"Maybe you really should stay here. Go back to your parents. You're still more a kid than a grownup anyway," Matt said.

"What's that supposed to mean?" Jim interrupted.

"I don't mean about this morning, but in other ways. The way you talk, for instance."

"And how do I talk?"

"You're always saying, 'I mean, after all, for chrissake.' Stuff like that. It's kid stuff. It gets on my nerves after a while. You're nothing but a kid. I almost wish I never met you."

"I guess I never knew how sensitive and mature your ears were!" Coming to Matt and standing directly in front of him, Jim continued: "I'll try to be careful of the way I talk since you listen so closely. I mean, after all, for chrissake, I don't want to hurt your ears or make you think I'm only a kid." Jim emphasized each of his words and glared directly into Matt's eyes.

"Then decide for yourself," Matt answered. "If you want to come with me, fine. I'll be back with the car. If not, leave whenever you want. Make up your own mind. At this point, I guess I really don't give a damn what you do."

Without stopping to see Jim's reaction, Matt left the house to begin his five-mile hike to the church. He went down his driveway and began walking along the berm of the country road.

Less than half a mile from his front gate, Matt looked to the distant hillside where old man Caffrey lived. And beyond that farm, the full view of the village cemetery came into sight. Nothing was distinct from such a distance, but the entire cemetery impressed itself on Matt. He kept walking while his eyes burned in the afternoon sunshine.

The bleating of sheep provided the only distraction. Mr. McCutchin, Matt's neighbor, had a flock of several hundred and few even bothered to watch as Matt walked along the road. The sheep continued to graze and bleat without interruption. Mr. McCutchin, standing near his barn, noticed Matt walking on the road, and raised his arm to wave.

It wasn't often Matt walked on this road; generally he was in his car. The longer he walked, the more his attention turned to the countryside itself. With its hills and dales, hollows and cliffs, and large open vistas, the country was beautiful, there was no denying that.

Matt broke his stride abruptly. He hesitated, looking back to his farm.

He began walking again, but this time with quickened pace. His steps were taken with resolution.

When he came within sight of the church his heart began pounding. He stayed among the trees at the river's edge till he saw his parked car.

Sweat ran off his forehead into his eyes and he was ready to make a run for the car, when the doors to the church basement opened and a stream of children came rushing out for recess. They were laughing and shouting and squealing. Marie was amid them like a mother hen clucking over her brood. Greg was with the children. Matt watched his son running around the churchyard with the other children. Their words could not be distinguished but the innocent sounds of their giggling carried far beyond the church property.

Matt waited. Less than fifteen minutes passed. Then the children returned to the church basement. After they disappeared behind its doors Matt rose from the crouched position in which he had been hiding and he hurried down the road toward the parking lot. Stealing between the parked cars, he came down to his '68 Chevy, got in, started the motor, and drove from the lot.

Arriving back home, he hurried through the house to his bedroom to throw some clothing together. Not until he began packing did he suddenly stand still and call out.

"You in here, Jim?"

Matt stopped pulling clothes from his closet and waited for an answer. None came.

"Jim! You here?"

Only silence.

Matt sat on the edge of the bed and looked at the clothes he had pulled from the closet.

He didn't move till the creaking floorboards alerted him to someone else's presence in the house.

"You about ready?" Jim asked.

"Where have you been?"

"Took a walk. Way beyond the barn. Wanted to take one last look at the valley and countryside. Probably won't see it again. By the time you get back to Marie I'll be packing off for college. Get out of this goddam Willow Glen once and for all."

Matt got off the bed.

"I don't want you to stop at my house so I'll have to share your clothes," Jim said. "We're the same size."

Matt looked deeply into Jim's eyes.

"You sure about what you're doing?" Matt asked.

"I know. I thought about it. Long before today."

"What if your father says I made you come?"

Jim reached into his rear pocket and pulled out a wallet. He flipped it open and pointed to a small block on a card.

"See this?" Jim asked. "It's my birthdate. I'm eighteen already and I'll be nineteen on November eleventh. I'm old enough to live my own life. Anyway, can you imagine what it would be like living with my father from now on?"

While Jim rummaged through the closet and bureau drawers to get some clothes for himself, Matt sat at the kitchen table, writing a note to his wife.

> Dear Marie,
>
> You may not believe it if I say I'm sorry, but I am. Not for the way I feel about Jim. But you'd probably never understand that.
>
> I'm sorry for the way you must feel. But I know that for now, it's best that I leave. I need some time for myself. You'll hear from me soon. Believe me, Marie, I didn't intend to hurt you.
>
> Matt

He held the note in his hand and read it several times.

"Here," Matt said as he handed the paper to Jim. "What do you think?"

Jim gave Matt a puzzled look as he accepted the paper and began reading.

"It's all right, I guess," Jim said. "What else can you say? How the hell am I supposed to know what a married man should write on a note to his wife when he's leaving her for another man?"

As soon as he said it, Jim raised his left hand to his mouth. He nervously coughed as he rubbed his hand over his lips.

"Here, give me that note again so I can read it," Jim said. "Maybe I'll have an idea."

Jim silently mouthed every word as he carefully read the note.

"I know how much you think of Greg. Maybe you could say something on the note about him," Jim suggested.

Jim waited as Matt added a postscript at the bottom of the sheet: "P.S. Tell Greg I love him and I'll see him soon."

The note was placed on the kitchen table under a saltshaker.

They left the bedroom, and while Jim continued through the hallway Matt stepped into Marie's bedroom. He went inside and picked up the family photograph sitting on the bureau.

"Are you coming?" Jim called.

Matt was about to place the picture in his bag, but he returned the photograph to its place on the bureau.

They left the house and moved to the car.

"By the way," Jim said, "while you were getting your car I put my bike in your barn."

"Don't you want it?"

"When we come back in the next couple days I'll get it... and if I don't get it then, Greg will find it someday. He can have it. Man, that bike's been ridden by a string of losers. Hope it doesn't rub off on Greg."

Matt didn't answer as he looked from Jim's face to the barn.

Once the clothing was thrown on the back seat of the car they were ready to leave.

Matt's eyes moved from right to left as they coasted down the driveway to the road.

"Do you think this is one of those things I'll live to regret?" Matt asked.

Matt glanced over at Jim on the passenger side.

"Were you satisfied living with Marie?"

Matt made no answer.

9

"Know where you're going?" Jim asked.

"Not really," Matt answered. "So long as I get away from Willow Glen. Get lost in a crowd. Need some time to sort things out."

After driving to Junction 235, Matt stopped the car and studied both directions.

"Turn right," Jim suggested impulsively.

Matt obeyed without question.

"Do you have any money?" Jim asked. "I've only got a couple bucks."

"Enough for a few days. That's all. I'll probably be back home by the time my money runs out. Only need a day or two for myself."

The '68 Chevy rattled along the highway in the far right lane as semi-trailer rigs and foreign imports cruised past Matt's car. The speed of the traffic seemed to reflect Matt's life. He questioned whether his whole life was not as much out of sync with the rest of the world as his car. Around the farm and countryside the car provided the transportation he needed. On the interstate it was ungainly and outdated.

After several hours they stopped at a diner along the highway. Two truckers sat at two separate tables and a teenage couple huddled in one of the booths along the side wall. Matt and Jim sat at a small table some distance from the others while they waited for the waitress to prepare their hamburgers and drinks. Music from the jukebox rumbled through the floor.

"While we're waiting for the food, want to dance?" Jim asked.

"Are you crazy? In front of all these people? What would they say? Anyway, I've never danced with a man in my life."

Jim started tapping his fingers on the table in rhythm with the jukebox.

"Get a load of that girl," Jim said. "Over there – the teenager."

Matt casually turned his head in her direction.

"What about her?" Matt asked.

"Braces. Reminds me of Ellen."

Matt smiled.

Silence followed.

"Not very crowded," Jim said.

"Off night. Middle of the week. Won't get many farm people out on a night in the middle of the week."

"Oh.'"

"Mostly truckers," Matt explained.

"Get a load of that one over there."

"Which one?"

"The one with the mustache," Jim said. "I like hair."

The comment brought Matt's eyes to Jim.

"That's one of the things I like about you," Jim continued.

"That'll be four dollars and eighty cents, please." The waitress handed a sack to Matt and slashed a toothy smile at Jim. A year or so younger than Matt, she let her eyes rove over Matt as he sorted out the correct change in his hand.

"My girlfriend and I get off work in an hour, if you and your buddy want to wait around."

"Should we wait?" Jim asked as he turned to Matt and winked.

Matt's mouth opened slightly in surprise.

"They've got a late movie down at the North Star Drive-In. Maybe the four of us could go see it," the waitress encouraged.

"Sounds like a great idea to me," Jim said.

The cheeks of the waitress flushed with excitement.

Together with Matt and Jim, the waitress went to the cashier's table while the bill was being paid.

Matt and Jim stood side by side at the counter.

"Only one thing," Jim said.

"What's that?" the waitress giggled.

"You and your girlfriend will have to sit together in the back seat so me and Matt can sit together."

Matt smiled and lifted his hand to the counter to couple his fingers round Jim's hand.

The blushing smile vanished from the face of the waitress.

"Why is it always me? This morning the toilet in my house overflowed, this afternoon the muffler on my car fell off, and now this. Forget it, fellas; I'm not that hard up." She brusquely walked away and was shaking her head as she walked into the kitchen.

Jim was still laughing as he walked to the car.

"You handled that like a pro," he said.

Matt smiled.

"Want me to drive a while?" Jim asked.

"I'd rather not. Driving keeps my mind off Marie and Greg."

They got in the car and eased onto the interstate.

About ten o'clock that night a soft glow rose on the horizon which slowly grew, both in breadth and intensity, as they continued on the highway. Together with the glow there was a steadily increasing amount of traffic on both sides of the median.

Jim, who had been dozing off and on for the past several hours, awakened and stared into the darkness. A large, illuminated roadsign listed the distances to cities that lay ahead and when he saw it a soft whistle escaped his lips.

"If this clunker can make it another twenty miles, we're in luck. It's where my dad was pastor when I was in high school. I know the place. I've got friends there who'll put us up overnight. That's why I directed you this way, but I didn't know if your rattletrap would make it or not."

For Matt, it was the first good news all day. It didn't make the car move any faster but it provided some hope.

Once they reached the roadsign marking the city limits, Jim gave explicit directions. Leaving the highway on Exit 39, Matt found himself in the heart of the city. Following Jim's directions, Matt drove through the city streets into the fringes of a business district.

This section of the city was old.

Small grocery stores and business establishments stood at the corners of blocks of houses. The size of the houses made Matt think that at one time it was an upper-class district of the city. But now the large houses had signs stuck in front yards indicating that they were no longer single-family dwellings. "Clean rooms." "Duplex to rent." "Rooms: Week or Month." Signs chronicled the recent history of the once fashionable neighborhood.

"This next street," Jim said suddenly. "Turn right."

Matt, not expecting a sudden turn, squealed the brakes as he slowed to round the corner.

"Now, don't go too fast... down there in the next block."

Matt trustfully obeyed the directions.

"Here," Jim hollered, pointing to an old, rambling brick house.

Jim was out of the car before Matt turned off the ignition. While he was standing on the sidewalk the front door of the house opened and two young men came down the porch steps.

"Is that you, Jim?" one yelled in disbelief.

"Willie?"

There was no moon and it was difficult to distinguish anyone's features under the dim streetlight but Jim and Willie recognized one another. Willie grabbed Jim around the back and hugged him so hard that Jim was almost thrown off his balance.

"What brings you back here? I thought you moved out to the sticks with the hicks," Willie laughed.

"Keep it down, Willie. Matt's from Willow Glen."

Willie stepped forward, grabbed Matt's hand, and shook it vigorously.

"Oh! A farmer!" Willie said to Matt. "Nothing personal but I knew there wouldn't be enough meat on the farm to satisfy Renalski."

Willie winked at Matt.

"Uh, my farm is mostly in grain," Matt answered seriously. "Only a few head of cattle. But old man McCutchin down the road has a big flock of sheep."

"Huh?" Willie exclaimed. "What's he talking about?"

"Hey," Jim quickly interrupted, "we don't have anywhere to stay tonight. Do they still have the rooms upstairs?"

"Yeah. Yeah... sure," Willie said. "Will you be here a couple days?"

"Probably. Maybe longer. I don't know yet," Jim said. "Why?"

"Let's get together," Willie said. "Like old times, huh? You and me and Matt and Earl. Hey, you never met Earl. Come over here, Earl. I want you to meet somebody I've known for years and years and years."

Earl was clearly not talkative. Nor was he impressed with meeting Jim and Matt.

Introductions were made, cool greetings exchanged, then both Earl and Matt backed away, in opposite directions.

"When can we get together?" Willie insisted.

"I really don't know, Willie. Maybe tomorrow sometime. I don't know. We may not even be in town that long. I don't know."

"We'll see," Willie said. "I'd really like to get together."

"Maybe," Jim said tentatively.

Matt watched Jim and Willie kiss each other in parting, and then he saw Willie and Earl walk down the street, hand in hand.

"Do you see that?" Matt said.

"What?" Jim answered.

"Willie's holding hands with Earl. In public. And he kissed you. In public. Right out here on the street."

"So," Jim muttered.

"You never told me Willie was a... a homosexual."

"What do you think I am? And what do you think you are?"

The questions appeared to startle Matt who remained standing on the sidewalk as Jim made his way onto the front porch.

The imposing structure was of brick, its gables and garrets laden with the gingerbread decorations of the late nineteenth century. An iron railing separated the narrow front yard from the sidewalk and led to a flight of stone steps up to the deep front porch.

Not until they reached the front door, dimly lit by a solitary low-wattage bulb, did Matt speak.

"Where are we? Whose house are we at? Do Willie's parents live here?"

Jim pointed to a small neatly lettered sign under the lighted bulb:

THE CENTER
TEMPORARY SHELTER – 24-HOUR COUNSELING
GAY MEN

"Aw, for chrissake!" Matt grumbled. He turned his back to Jim and shuffled several paces away where he put his hands in his hip pockets and stared up at the sky.

"I thought only kids said that," Jim remarked sarcastically.

"Why did you drag me here?" Matt demanded.

Jim cocked his head to one side and looked at Matt.

"OK," Jim said. "Let's get back in the car!"

"I thought you said you knew some people in this city. Why can't we stay with them?" Matt asked.

"These are the people!" Jim said. "And this is the place!"

"Aw, for chrissake," Matt repeated.

"If you're so proud, maybe we should go to the Terrace Plaza downtown. They have a honeymoon suite on the twenty-eighth floor. Maybe it's vacant tonight."

Matt stepped to the railing enclosing the front porch and clamped his hands on the cold metal. He looked through the darkness to the ground below. Finally he turned to Jim: "Okay. But only for one night."

Jim opened the door and Matt followed him into a large room that opened off the front entry hall. Matt had the distinct feeling he was back home in Willow Glen at the Tyler Brothers' Funeral Parlor. It even looked like their place. Only the flowers and guest register were missing. High ceilings and massive amounts of wood paneling in the house offered the same distinctive appearance as the Tyler place: beamed ceilings, wainscoting, crown molding, wide floorboards, woodwork of walnut, oak, ash, and cherry. The expensive wood, scratched and worn with age, belonged to another era.

A middle-aged man rose from the sofa and came to Jim as soon as he saw him. He was dressed casually – gray slacks and a light blue, short-sleeved shirt. The man's hairline was receding and traces of gray throughout his hair were conspicuous, but he moved with the agility of a much younger man. His face was full, but scarcely fat, and a disarming smile covered it when he came toward them. The man leaned forward and kissed Jim gently on the lips.

"Jim. It's good to see you again." The man's voice was deep, his words enunciated distinctly. "I didn't expect to see you so soon."

If not by introduction, then by manner, Matt knew the man was in charge.

"My plans changed a little," Jim stammered. "I'll tell you about it later.... Richard, I'd like you to meet Matt."

Matt extended his hand in greeting.

"Richard," Jim began, "we need a place to stay tonight. Maybe for a couple days. Any room here?"

"Stay as long as you like," Richard said. "I think Room 33 is open."

Matt watched Richard cautiously and his eyes continued to survey his new environment suspiciously.

"You know the policy," Richard reminded. "Stay here for a couple days till you get your feet on the ground; then, if you're able, make a small payment for your room after you've landed a job."

"We won't be here that long," Matt broke in. "A day or two at the most."

"Fine," Richard answered quietly. "Whatever you say."

The conversation turned to small talk. Richard diplomatically avoided asking any questions. After the formalities of introduction and assignment of room, Jim and Matt went to the car to retrieve their clothing from the back seat. Neither spoke.

They returned to the house, their arms piled with their garments. Matt followed Jim through the entry hall past the telephone to the stairway. Reaching the landing on the second floor, Jim motioned with a nod of his head to the third floor. When they got there Jim looked for Room 33 and after finding the number on a door, he opened it and walked in to find a room furnished with spartan simplicity. Two cots, a nightstand, and a small desk lamp were the major furnishings. A single chair separated the cots. The desk lamp provided the only light, so the room remained dimly shadowed. The room was clean but worn with use. The oppressive, darkly varnished woodwork was another era's notion of good taste. Matt tapped the door with curiosity; solid core doors had become cost-prohibitive in most house construction long ago.

Matt followed on the heels of Jim as though he was a youngster afraid of getting lost. Time had not yet begun to blunt the feelings he experienced earlier in the day, nor was his new environment contributing to any sense of ease.

"Is there a bathroom in this place?" Matt asked.

"Down the hallway," Jim volunteered. "Last room on the left."

When Matt walked down the hallway he saw two or three men in different rooms but they gave the impression of having recently arrived to spend the night. They made no effort to speak with Matt, nor he with them.

Matt's attention was drawn to another room. Someone inside was crying. Matt walked to the open doorway, paused, and looked inside. A teenager was sitting on the bed, sobbing uncontrollably. Seated beside him was a man in his late twenties. The older man's arm was round the shoulder of the youth, trying to comfort him. When the youth looked up, Matt saw that his left eye was almost swollen shut. Matt stared at the scene before him.

"What happened?" Matt asked. "Can I help?"

The man in his twenties spoke. "As soon as I get him calmed down a little, we'll go over to the emergency room at the hospital and have them patch up his eye. It seems his father found out tonight that he has a gay son. The boy got kicked out of his house, but not before his father roughed him up. The father told him never to come back. Then, the kid went to his parish priest for help. The priest was flip. He told the kid his church honors angels, not fairies, and ordered the kid off church property. We got him here about an hour ago. Nearly suicidal."

"But... they shouldn't have... will the kid... what will you...."

Matt's loss for words was apparent.

"Don't worry about it, buddy," the man in his twenties said. "We know how to handle this kind of situation. In another couple hours we'll have him settled down a little. He needs a good night's sleep. Then tomorrow we'll help him put his life back together. At least we'll start. The scars from tonight will be there a long, long time. But we've helped others like him."

Matt walked away from the room and continued down the hallway.

Matt stepped behind the door clearly marked "Restroom," and the inside, although not spacious, was certainly larger than most home bathrooms. In addition to the enclosure for a toilet, there was a urinal, a shower stall, and a sink. The soap dispenser on the wall beside the sink was filled to the top and the wall mirror above the sink was free of any water spots. It sparkled. The black and white checkerboard floor was as clean as hundred-year-old marble can be and the white porcelain sink shone brightly.

Two young men stood by the sink. A trickle of blood ran from the mouth of one, while the other applied a compress to his lip. They ignored Matt and spoke only with each other.

"You're lucky he only hit you in the mouth," the one said excitedly. "I remember one night when he followed me. I spent the next day at the hospital getting my finger put back together. He broke it. Right in two. Here I thought he was gay. Following me out of the bar and all. But it turned out he's a stomper. I wish all the nice little bashers would stay in their own homophobic bars and beat up each other."

"If he doesn't want to go out with other guys, then why does he hang around the Golden Peacock? I don't understand some people."

"The doll who came to my rescue was the type I dream about. I swear to God, he was pretty. Gorgeous is more like it."

"From a distance I always thought he was young. He really does have such a pretty face and those shirts he wears always look like they're ready to rip apart every time he takes a deep breath."

"Up close, though, you can see crow's-feet all around his eyes."

"I know. That's exactly what I thought."

"And did you ever look at his arms? They're always beautifully tanned, but they're getting that crinkled, drawn, midlife look. Have you ever had the chance to look at his hand – the skin between his wrist and thumb? It's all rippled like alligator's skin. Too much sun. Not enough oil. That'll do it every time."

"How old is he?"

"Pretty ancient, I think. Bristly hairs stick out of his ears and nose so I suspect he's thirty. Maybe even thirty-five."

"God, I wonder what keeps them going once they're that old!"

Matt listened to the two while he stood at the urinal. Not until he tried to wash his hands at the sink did the unhurt one speak to him.

"Would you help me for a minute?" the stranger asked Matt. "Look. Timmy needs medication for his mouth and I have to run downstairs to get some. His mouth won't stop bleeding. If you have the time, would you hold these cold cloths on his cut? Besides, he could use the company. Be a sweetie and help."

"Huh?" Matt mumbled.

"Be a jewel and help a brother."

With that, the compress was shoved into Matt's hand and the young man rushed out the door.

Timmy, the one whose mouth was bleeding, stood looking at Matt with large brown eyes. "Can you tell me something?" he asked. "Can you tell me why someone would try to bloody my face? All I did was walk into the bar. He saw me walking out. And blooey! Before I know what in holy heaven is happening, he bangs his fist right into my mouth. Jesus, Mary, and Joseph! I swear, I'll never understand some people."

Matt continued to apply pressure to the stranger's mouth as the trickle of blood slowed to a few isolated drops, and then, the final drop began to dry on the swollen lip.

"I'm not pushing this cloth against your mouth too hard, am I?" Matt asked.

"Oh, dear me, no! Just having your hand next to my face makes it feel better. Mercy, it feels good!"

The stranger's eyes moved from Matt's eye-level down past his chest and stopped slightly below his belt.

"If you've lived in this city very long, how have you managed to stay out of my sight?"

"I only arrived in the city about a half hour ago. I'm from Willow Glen."

"A refugee from the boonies! Absolutely marvelous! My friend – he's the one who went after the salve – is staying at my apartment tonight. You can come with us. Oh, mercy me, I didn't mean that as a double entendre, but... you *can* come with us. The three of us can have a delicious time. You'll love my friend – well, not too much, I hope! Earlier this evening we picked up some reefers and we'll share."

"Uh... thanks anyway, but I came into town with... uh, my boyfriend...."

"Your boyfriend?" the stranger cried out. "Oh dear, that hurt my lip to laugh. But golly gompers, I think that's the first time I ever heard that. Your boyfriend. You're really cute. I mean it. If you can't visit the apartment tonight, maybe some other time. I'm here at The Center all the time. The Center sponsors socials, picnics, card parties, lectures, potlucks. We just do oodles of things. My name's Timmy."

The stranger's friend returned with a small tube of ointment that he rubbed generously over the cut. Again, the two ignored Matt as they spoke with each other in animated gestures.

Matt walked out of the bathroom and down the corridor. At Room 33 he quietly turned the doorknob. Jim was lying in bed with his eyes closed. Matt stepped back into the hallway, softly pulled the door closed again, and walked down the steps to the first floor. Fumbling for some coins in his pocket, he stopped at the wall telephone near the front door.

After he dialed he heard the phone ringing at the other end of the line. It was not long before someone picked up the receiver.

"Hello," Matt said, then paused.

"Yeah, it's me. I only wanted to call and hear whether you got home from Bible camp all right."

A frown covered his face as he listened.

"What was I supposed to do? It's my car, too. What more do you want?"

He waited and listened as Marie spoke.

"It's too late to change any of that now. I only wanted to tell you there's enough money in the bank account to get yourself a car. We need another one anyway. There's not nearly enough for a new one, but you can get a used car as good as the old Chevy."

The frown returned to Matt's face as he listened.

"Suit yourself. You'll do what you want anyway.... Yeah, we're together. He helped me find a place to stay... I don't know the address."

Matt called to someone sitting in the living room to ask the address. He repeated it to Marie over the phone.

"I don't know how long we'll be here. A day. Maybe two days. It all depends. I don't want you running around telling people I deserted you and abandoned Greg.... Huh?"

Matt listened.

"A month or so ago you and Greg stayed over at your folks for a week. Can't I have a vacation too? The only difference between what you did and what I'm doing is that what I'm doing came up all of a sudden. I decided on the spot that I needed to get away for a couple days."

His grip on the receiver tightened as he again listened.

"So what? Jim just decided to come along with me. I didn't force him into it. The truth is, I tried to get him to go back home.... What? I know how hard it'll be for you to face people. Maybe I shouldn't have, but–"

Marie spoke for some time.

"You're the one who told that damn preacher. If you'd kept your mouth shut, the two of us could have worked things out.... Of course I miss Greg.... Is he all right?"

Suddenly Matt held the receiver away from his ear. All he heard was the loud hum of the dial tone. He slammed the receiver down on its cradle and headed for the stairs.

"Want to join us?" a voice called to Matt.

Richard was standing in the doorway to one of the back rooms in the house. Matt followed Richard into a small room beside the kitchen on the first floor.

When the house was originally built, the room may have served as an informal dining room, judging from its placement next to the kitchen. Now, bookshelves on two sides of the room suggested it was used as a conference or reading room.

Three other men, all dressed casually, were already sitting in the room. Matt felt out of place. He still wore the white T-shirt and faded blue denim pants he wore when he left Willow Glen. Apart from seeing Matt, the men continued their conversation without interruption.

"Since the divorce I see them once a week," one of the men was saying. "The judge allowed me several hours every Sunday afternoon. I had to fight like the devil to get those couple hours. I don't have any problems with the kids. Sometimes she gives me a hard time, but what can I do. She always was a bitch." The words came from a man whom Matt judged to be in his early thirties. His clothing appeared expensive but compared to Matt's faded farm clothes, anything would have looked expensive.

"Well," said another, "my wife and I separated on friendly terms. It was at her insistence that I have as many visitation rights as I do. Really, it wasn't because I'm gay that we separated. We merely grew apart. She had her career; I had mine. It was too much of a hassle living together anymore. I'm glad we live in a fairly tolerant neighborhood. It's a cosmopolitan cross section and the neighbors accept it as a matter of fact that no two people are alike. It's easier on the kids. Word gets around, you know. And my kids are Class-A blabbermouths. They're not bothered that their old man's gay and they don't hesitate telling other kids. Sometimes I think they're even proud of their old man. But it was becoming inconvenient. While my wife was out of town on business, I'd have Todd sleep over with me. And my wife hired a secretary – called Rhonda, or Rhoda, or Rhea; hell, I don't know her name – but she was often at the house when I wasn't. Then the three kids and their friends were running around the house all the time. Good grief, it was like the check-out counter at a discount store. People all over the place all the time. So, my wife and I just separated. I think she's got something going with that secretary, anyway. But they make a nice couple. And now that I've moved in with Todd, life's much better for everyone. Last month when Todd and I went to Europe to close that electronics deal we even took the kids along. Did they ever have fun!"

Matt sat to one side of the room, listening as the men continued talking. His eyes passed from one to the other as the men talked about divorces, separations, custody rights, and being gay. He was used to the conversations the farmers had in Willow Glen: spring planting, the county fair, fall harvests, the price of corn, and how to fatten hogs.

"I see you're married," one of the men said to Matt, pointing to the wedding band on his finger.

"I used to be... I mean I am... that is, until today. Well, I'm still married. I'm just not home tonight." Matt's stuttering caused all eyes in the room to turn in his direction. Richard broke the tension.

"It sounds as though you've had an interesting day," Richard said.

Matt glanced at his finger and the simple, gold wedding band.

"I heard there's an old Chinese curse," another put in. "If you want to curse someone, you tell him you hope all his days are interesting."

"Didn't mean it that way," Richard explained.

In an uncharacteristic and spontaneous flood of words, Matt recounted the events that occurred earlier in the day. When he finished he felt embarrassed to have told complete strangers what he hesitated even to *think* about. The men in the room heard him out and made no effort to interrupt. Not until he finished and let a blank stare cover his face, did anyone speak.

"At least your wife was lucky that she found out directly. My wife read about me in the newspaper. I tried to stay in the closet; thought no one would know. I met some guy in a bookstore. We went to a backroom. When I was all set to go, he pulls out a badge. I was, well, becoming friendly with a cop. Believe me, it's easier on your nerves to jump out of that closet and be honest with yourself."

"Were you ever married?" one of the men asked Richard.

"No," he said. "Never had the desire."

"That's the way to go," said another. "I wish that thirty years ago when my old man tried to tell me about the birds and the bees, he would have known as much about what he called the queers and the perverts. Man, did he have a mess of misinformation. Had he known more, it would certainly have spared me anguish and rough times when I tried to marry and live as a straight. I thought I was the only homosexual who ever lived."

"It's really strange talking to you men," Matt blurted out. "I've only talked with you for a half hour but I feel like I've known you all my life. It's weird. I've never had this feeling talking to a group of men before. It's like for the first time in my life, I've found people who understand me. Oh, there's Jim. Sure. But I thought it was something unique between the two of us."

"What are you doing down here?" The words came from someone at the doorway. "I was looking all over the place for you," Jim said.

Forgetting the others in the room, Matt got off his chair and followed Jim out into the hallway.

"After I called Marie, Richard asked me to join the others for a while."

"Marie? A phone call?" Jim shouted. "You mean you called her? You actually called your wife from here? You didn't tell her where we are, did you?"

"Yeah. Why not?"

"Why not?" Jim yelled. "If she tells my father he'll be on our necks as soon as he can get here."

Matt looked at Jim in bewilderment.

10

Force of habit opened Matt's eyes before sunrise next morning. His first impulse was to plan the work schedule for the day. But then reality crowded his mind. There would be no farm work today. Exhaustion, rather than contentment, caused him to sleep throughout the night and now the uncertainty of his future lay ahead. Sneaking away from the farm was easy. Leaving the painful prospects behind was convenient. But now realistic consequences had to be faced.

He turned his head on the pillow till he was looking out the small window in the room. Only the solid brick wall of an adjoining house some twenty feet away was visible. He laid in bed, restlessly tossing from side to side and wishing that Jim would awaken but it was almost eight o'clock before Jim's eyes opened. Only then did Matt get dressed.

The Center was quiet as Matt walked down the two flights of steps to the small kitchen at the rear of the house. Either everyone was still sleeping or they had all left the house.

When Matt stepped into the kitchen Richard was sitting at the table. The morning paper was spread out before him.

"Sleep well?"

"In fits. As well as could be expected," Matt answered.

Richard folded the paper and tossed it on a chair beside him.

"After you rest today, you'll feel better," Richard said.

"Can't do that. I haven't sat around doing nothing for the whole of my life. I'm not starting today. I did a lot of thinking through the night."

Richard allowed several moments to pass.

"Did I get the impression last evening that you would only be in town for a couple days?" Richard said.

"Jim can go back home to his parents whenever he wants. But I'm not going back to Marie."

"That's a big step," Richard said. "Have you thought it all the way through?"

"I've made the break. And for now, at least, I need some time away from her. And that means more than two or three days. Maybe in a couple weeks I'll go back. Maybe a couple months. But not now."

"Who'll do your farm work?" Richard asked.

"Marie's brothers and father," Matt answered.

"Just like that," Richard said, snapping his fingers. "You're unloading all your work on somebody else?"

"Whose goddam side are you on?" Matt said angrily.

Richard raised his eyebrows.

"Of course I've thought about that," Matt said. "And it makes me feel guilty as hell. But what am I supposed to do? Go back and face that preacher and that town? They'd crucify me. I know it."

Richard traced his index finger along the colored lines embossed on the tablecloth. His eyes remained downcast.

"Any immediate plans?" Richard asked.

"Get a job so I can live and send Marie some money every week for herself and Greg. Can't send her much, but it's not my intention to abandon either her or Greg. I'll just have to get a job."

"Where?"

"I don't know."

"What can you do?"

"That's a laugh. I'm a farmer. Know of any big farms here in the city?"

"Maybe."

Matt looked at Richard skeptically.

"Maybe not a farm as such, but I may be able to help you get something."

Jim walked into the room and immediately went about getting his breakfast.

Richard got off his chair and left the room. A couple of minutes later he was back in the room carrying a leather folder at least two inches thick. He began thumbing through the sheets and finally, a third of the way through the stack, he stopped and pulled out a sheet.

"Do you mind cutting grass?" Richard asked.

"Wouldn't that be a step up in the world," Matt said disgustedly.

"It's something," Richard said. "A start."

"Matt has all sorts of skills," Jim interrupted. "He can do carpentry work, mechanical repairs, roofing – he doesn't have to cut grass."

"Why didn't you say so, Matt?" asked Richard.

Richard returned the sheet of paper to the folder and again began paging through the rest of the stack. Finally he came upon another which he pulled out.

"Here we go. The Division of Parks is looking for a maintenance supervisor with all-around skills. Sort of a jack-of-all-trades. I know they've been looking for a couple weeks, and there's no one with the experience and skills to take the job. Want to look into it?"

After reading the job description, Matt reached for a pencil to copy the address and phone number of the place.

"I'll check into it."

Jim turned from the refrigerator and came to the table beside Matt.

"Maybe I overslept but I get the feeling I missed out on something important. Aren't you going back to Willow Glen in a day or two?"

"That was my original plan. But I changed my mind."

A broad grin covered Jim's face.

"So you're not going back to Marie, huh?"

"I got a couple extra bucks," Matt said. "I'll buy a bus ticket so you can return to Willow Glen."

"Not on your life," Jim laughed.

"But if I get this job," Matt said, waving the job description, "what will you do? And I'll tell you this. Even if I don't get this job, I'm not returning to Marie or Willow Glen. Certainly not now, at least."

"No problem," said Jim. "I know some people here in town. They'll help me get something if I ask. Willie works over at the hospital. Maybe he'll help me get something."

"You want to go with me to apply for this job?" Matt asked Jim.

"Bad business," Richard said immediately. "An employer doesn't like it if somebody tags along with you."

They made arrangements for the day. While Matt would apply for the job with the park district, Jim would set out to find a place where he and Matt might stay for the next few weeks. Soon after finishing breakfast, both set out on their respective tasks for the day. They agreed to meet back at The Center no later than six o'clock.

That evening, the grandfather clock in the hallway of The Center was chiming a quarter past six when Jim came huffing into the room.

"I began to think you weren't coming back," Matt called from a chair in the large room.

"Get the job?" Jim asked immediately.

"Start tomorrow," Matt answered.

"Good, you can pay the rent."

"Get an apartment?" Matt asked.

"Finding somewhere to stay in the city is almost impossible, but I finally got a place," Jim said. "It's not much – the top half of a duplex – but it'll do for now. It's furnished. I guess you'd call it that – with some chairs and a big double bed. Small kitchen, too."

"When can we move in?"

"Tonight, if you want," Jim said quickly. "I want to get out of here as soon as possible. Get to another address."

"What's the rush?" Matt asked.

"So my dad won't find us."

"You're paranoid. Always afraid that he's out to get you."

"You may call it paranoid. But I've been living with my father for eighteen years. I know how he fought gay men in this city. And believe me, when he says he's opposed to gay rights, you better believe him. It's not me who's paranoid. He is – about gay people. He thinks we're plotting to destroy the world."

Matt looked at Jim but didn't answer.

They loaded their clothes back into the car. "You know the city," Matt said, handing Jim the car keys. "You drive."

Jim grinned and moved toward the car door on the driver's side.

He drove toward the western side of the city. The sun was setting directly in front of them but only a small reddish sliver could be glimpsed above the tall buildings cluttering the city and the blue sky that had overhung the city by day was now deepening to indigo.

"Man, this is a wild part of the city," Jim said.

"How's that?"

"You're kidding! Surely somebody back at The Center mentioned Fifteenth Street," Jim insisted.

Fifteenth Street stretched two miles across town and its eastern end was known to many in the city. The police knew it well. As the car bumped across several sets of railroad tracks jutting like rickety bones above the ill-paved street, Matt felt that he was passing into another city. Most of the buildings, squatted close to the concrete sidewalks, were two stories tall and crowded so tightly one upon the other that only scavenging cats and stray dogs had room to squeeze between them. Run-down laundromats, down-at-heel grocery stores, and abandoned buildings with smashed windowpanes lined this end of Fifteenth Street. Adult bookstores dotted either side of the street and the flashing lights of peep show marquees flickered like modern-day votive candles in the ancient rites of Dionysus. Luridly colored bulbs, oscillating round the slogans of "Live Action – XXX-Rated," drew one's eyes to the establishments below. Thumb-sucking children with dirty faces and straggly hair appeared behind tattered curtains in some windows indicating that the red-light district was home to some who were not patrons.

"Do you suppose families actually live in these hovels?" Matt asked.

"I guess so. I see kids behind the windows."

"The kids. Look at them! They look like kids in concentration camps."

"So? Not everybody lives on a big spread in Willow Glen."

"Was there an accident or something?" Matt casually asked. "Why are all these people standing around?"

Jim laughed. "They're getting ready for work. That's all."

At the sound of their car moving along Fifteenth Street some young men turned and stuck out their thumbs for a lift. But most of the figures on the street were not walking. Their bodies were propped against the buildings. Some wore T-shirts; most were shirtless. With bodies stationary, expressions cloaked in blank stares, and eyes darting from one car to the next, they watchfully eyed the passing motorists.

Young men and boys were the rule in some blocks, young women and girls in others. As though by pre-arrangement and mutual consent, the blocks were segregated by gender.

Standing on the front step of a closed laundromat was a boy, not more than ten years old whose smooth cheeks had not yet known the scrape of a razor. His bare chest had not yet begun to fill out; he was barefoot. He had the palm of his hand spread over the crotch of his cut-off Levi's, and he consciously moved his fingers as his eyes beckoned each passing motorist. Jim stopped for a red light immediately beside the laundromat and when he did, the boy raised his hand to Matt. In answer, Matt raised his arm slightly and the boy started to approach the car.

"Man, what're you doing?" Jim asked.

As soon as the light turned green, Jim drove away from the intersection.

"He only waved and I waved back," Matt explained.

"Man, he's out hustling for the night."

"Hustling?"

"He's a chicken and thinks you're a hawk." Jim was stunned at Matt's naïveté.

"What did you call him?" Matt asked. "A hawk?"

"For chrissake," Jim exclaimed. "He's a chicken! A chicken! How much plainer do I have to say it? You know what hawks do to chickens," Jim said as he smacked his lips together with a slurping sound. "My gosh, Matt, I'll bet that ten-year-old kid knows more about street life and living in general than you do. Sometimes I wonder what cave you've been hiding in all your life. I really mean it, Matt, for chrissake."

Matt looked out the car window in disbelief.

"Kids that young?" Matt asked.

"You better believe it."

At the corner in the next block Jim spied a kid, maybe seventeen, leaning against the brick building. Searching the cars, his eyes were looking for one of his regulars or maybe a new customer.

"OK, Matt, if you want to see what Fifteenth Street's like, here's your chance."

Jim slowed the car and the kid carefully eyed the two. Jim almost brought the car to a stop in front of the kid, then slowly steered around the corner. The kid was alone and had no difficulty seeing the two occupants of the car.

As Jim drove around the corner he cautioned Matt. "Only open the window a crack. Only wide enough to talk to him, not wide enough that he can stick his hand inside the car. This is one of the most dangerous sections of the city."

Matt instinctively followed Jim's instructions. He cracked the window and within seconds the kid sauntered around the building and stooped to look inside the car.

"You cops? I ain't seen you guys here before."

The kid's breath reeked with alcohol.

"Yeah," Jim scowled. "FBI agents. We're advance men for a state visit by the Queen of England. She wants to do her wash in that laundromat. Hell," Jim demanded, "do we act like cops?"

"Well..." the kid stammered. "You guys lookin' for somethin' to do?"

"What d'ya have in mind?" Jim asked.

"Oh, I dunno. I'd like to make some bucks tonight. I'll do anythin' ya wanna do... but, ya gotta make it snappy. I've got a regular trick comin' by in 'bout fifteen minutes, and he doesn't like to wait. How many bucks ya got on ya?"

Jim decided the conversation had gone far enough.

"Well, buddy, we only got three bucks between us. How about taking all three?"

"Man," the kid replied, "you're nuts. I wouldn't even let ya feel it for three fuckin' bucks. Do it with two guys for three lousy bucks? You're either nuts or freaked out."

The kid stumbled away from the car and disappeared round the corner to resume his position against the building.

As they continued on Fifteenth Street Matt saw those people standing in doorways and on street corners. Prostitution and hustling. Teenage alcoholics and abandoned children. These were things he sometimes heard about on television but had never witnessed in Willow Glen. Now, however, as he saw the car ahead of theirs stop and a young boy get into it, he realized what was happening. It was so casual. So routine. So matter-of-fact.

"Is this what it's all about?" Matt asked.

"What do you mean?"

"The gay lifestyle? Is this what I'm getting myself into?"

"I guess that depends on what you choose. Sure, this is the lifestyle some gays choose. That's their business. I know other gays who don't choose this particular lifestyle. Don't stereotype, Matt. That's what homophobics do."

"Do you come down here very often?" Matt asked.

"Almost never. I drove this way tonight because it's a short-cut from the east to the west side of the city. But as far as coming down to Fifteenth Street to get my kicks – never. I don't need it. I just don't want it. It would take some major catastrophe in my life to ever make me come down here and walk Fifteenth Street. Even tonight, with you in the car with me, I'm anxious to get through this section."

Their car continued on Fifteenth Street past the Golden Peacock, a gay bar, and not far beyond a man was walking briskly down the sidewalk.

"Look over there," Jim said quickly.

As the car passed the man, he turned his back to enter a drugstore.

"I didn't see his face," Jim said, "but that was my dad! I know it! I'd recognize his walk anywhere. And that was his dark gray suit."

Matt turned his head quickly to catch a glimpse of the man's face, but the man had already disappeared into the drugstore.

"You're probably mistaken," Matt said. Then, after a pause, "Should we go back?"

"Not a chance."

"What harm could he do? And why would he be in this city?"

"To find me. You still won't believe my dad's homophobic, will you?" Jim asked.

Jim dropped the subject and continued driving away from the drugstore. He turned off Fifteenth Street and drove about two-and-a-half miles into a neighborhood where the houses were clustered closely together. Every house on the block appeared to be built from the identical architectural plan: two-story frame structure with wooden stairway on the right side of the house leading to a doorway on the second floor. The owners of the duplexes, silently refusing to conform with the imposed uniformity of the exteriors, affirmed their individuality with paintbrushes. On the farm, Matt was used to white houses with red barns. On this street, Matt saw every shade of the rainbow represented. Even in twilight the houses sparkled. And, as though to emphasize individuality even more dramatically, carefully painted murals decorated many front porches. The spectacle of so many identical houses decorated with such distinctive individuality caused an initial reaction of puzzlement.

"Winter home for the circus?" Matt commented, as he smiled.

"Livens up the street, doesn't it?"

In mock sarcasm, Matt asked: "Which tent is ours?"

"The light blue one with the crayfish painted on the front porch... upstairs."

Matt got out of the car and surveyed the street. The side windows between houses faced so close that one could crawl from house to house without ever entering a front door. Matt thought of the distances between farms in Willow Glen. Then, he looked at the blue house with the crayfish painted on the front porch. The sides of the house were almost touching its neighbors on either side.

Matt was impressed with the structural similarity of the houses, but he was even more taken with the tenants. Men were sitting on porches. Men were leaning out the windows talking to neighbors. Men were in the street tossing Frisbees. Men were talking on the sidewalk. There were no women to be seen. Men were everywhre. Some glanced toward Jim and Matt; some waved. But most went about their activities and ignored the presence of Matt and Jim. Not until Jim and Matt stepped onto the first wooden step leading to their rented duplex did anyone speak to them.

"Welcome," someone called out, "to the gay ghetto."

11

The final days of August, with their grass-brittle dryness and earth-hardened heat, drifted into the first week of September. As the September days slipped by, breezes pungent with the crisp aroma of autumn began to fill the air. Crackling leaves underfoot were reminders of the fading summer days. The change of seasons didn't mean much in the city; there, one heard about it on television. But on the farm, the arrival of autumn meant early morning dew on the grass, and Canadian geese flying overhead in their V-formation, and the ever-present odor in the air of chrysanthemums and pumpkins. Matt missed all this, and the tranquility and peace of the farm. But what he missed most was his son, Greg.

His life in the blue house with the crayfish murals became routine as his work with the park commission grew steady. Impressed with his work habits, Matt's boss gave him the awaited news: continued work throughout the winter months was guaranteed if Matt wanted it. His employment future was assured.

But his personal future remained uncertain. He called Marie once again. But when she answered and heard his voice, she hung up. Nor did she answer the one long letter he wrote. Even though he put his return address both on the envelope and at the top of the letter inside, she never answered. He never told Jim about the phone call, or the letter. Since arriving in the city, Matt had heard nothing of Greg.

When cashing his paycheck every other week, Matt sent Marie and Greg as much as he could afford. He didn't want to be accused of not supporting his wife and son. She never returned the checks, nor did she acknowledge their receipt beyond signing her endorsement on their reverse.

As far as Matt knew, Jim never tried to contact his parents.

And Jim did not start college. Getting a job as an orderly at City Hospital, Jim insisted he wanted some work experience before continuing his education. Matt felt responsible for that; guilty, too.

But this was Matt's routine by the end of September. His weekends and evening hours were predictable. He spent the evening by himself watching television while Jim worked the three-to-eleven shift at the hospital. By the time Jim got home at night, Matt was usually ready for bed. It was generally on Saturday and Sunday evenings that they went out together.

Such was the case on the last Saturday evening in September when, after eating, they made arrangements to go to The Center. It was dark outside, and past eight-thirty, when they made their way up the front sidewalk to the large brick building.

"I invited a doctor from the hospital over to our place sometime," Jim said. "I just found out today that he's gay. I think you'll like him. His name's Denison. Dr. Denison."

"You sure know a lot of people," Matt muttered as they stepped to the front door of The Center.

"So," Jim commented, "I like to circulate."

When Jim opened the front door, laughter and talking immediately drowned out all normal tones of conversation. The house was crowded and to be heard it was necessary to shout. Matt looked over the people and, as happened so many other times when he was in a group of gay men, he was surprised at all the new faces. There were a few regulars who showed up at almost every gathering, but generally, the faces were different. He'd see the people once, but not again; and he wondered where they came from and how they disappeared so completely.

Matt felt someone tapping him on the back as he looked around the crowd.

"Hey sweetie, I'll bet you don't remember me, do you?"

Matt turned. He saw an elfin creature smiling up at him. The young man was wearing a magenta silk shirt, its open placket forming a V beginning an inch or two above the navel and growing ever wider as it approached the shoulders. A medallion dangled from a golden chain round his neck, and as he flicked the ash from his cigarette in its long black holder, the medallion danced across his hairless chest between his rosebud nipples. The shirt sleeves were puffy at the elbows but skin-tight where three pearl-white buttons fastened the cuffs above the wrists. The white corduroy pants gave the impression of having been shrunk to fit by some new hermetic process which allowed no air pockets to remain. Every muscle, contour, and bulge was clearly defined.

"You're right," Matt hesitated. "I'm afraid I don't know you."

"Oh, dear me!" the young man moaned. "You were such an angel of mercy to me. Saint Francis of Assisi couldn't have been more compassionate. And now you don't even remember. I'm Timmy!"

He waited as Matt's eyes scanned his face.

"Upstairs!" Timmy cried. "The bathroom! My bloody mouth! You held a compress to it! You were such a gem. Mother Teresa wouldn't have been kinder."

"Oh, yeah... now I'm beginning to remember," Matt admitted. "You got beat up... I mean, somebody attacked you... I mean...."

"Oh, you silly goose! Here you remembered all the time," Timmy squealed with delight.

The noise in the room grew louder till quiet conversation became impossible. The pockets of people crowding the first floor were oddly separated from each other by glances. Matt felt some eyes looking through him and ignoring his very existence while others were slowly undressing him with their stares. Others nodded and smiled. Others spoke. The entry hall and large adjoining room were so crowded that not another person could have squeezed through the front door without a struggle.

Matt heard a familiar voice calling for attention. He finally saw Richard struggling to stand atop a straight-back chair.

"Please... please... you can party later. If I could have your attention for a few minutes."

Richard continued holding his arms up, asking for silence, but the roar in the room continued without break.

Timmy saw Richard's predicament and set about resolving it. Matt watched Timmy cup both hands beside his mouth. What followed was the highest pitched, most blood-curdling, banshee-like scream Matt had heard in his life.

Complete silence blanketed the room.

"Thank you, Timmy," said Richard.

"I have two announcements this evening. Some of you already know what I want to tell you," Richard started, "but I think it's important that all of you hear it. The elections are only about a month away. And Loren Pritchind is running for city council."

Catcalls and loud booing greeted Richard's remarks. He smiled and held up his arms to quiet the crowd.

"For your own protection," Richard continued, "we're advising you to study the candidates carefully."

"Pritchind," Matt mumbled to the person standing next to him. "I've heard that name somewhere."

"His name's plastered on billboards all over the city," the man answered.

"No," Matt insisted. "I've heard that name somewhere else, but I can't remember where."

"Now for the second announcement. And this news is more pleasant," Richard said. "There seems to be general agreement that this year one big Halloween Party would be better than many small ones all over the city."

A deafening roar of approval greeted Richard's remarks.

"So, we've already begun arrangements. It'll cost ten bucks a person."

Everybody booed – loud and long.

"But that entitles you to as much as you can eat and drink."

Wild cheering went up from the crowd.

"For those of you who drink too much, special provisions will be made to stay in the hall all night. Sleeping on the floor may not be comfortable, but it'll be safe."

Even louder yells of approval greeted this remark.

"You can buy your tickets in advance or at the door."

"Where will it be?" someone shouted.

"The Golden Moon. It's a party hall over on Sixty-Ninth Street."

Shouts of laughter followed Richard's announcement.

"You've got to be putting us on," somebody screamed.

Richard smiled and shook his head no. "That's what it's called and that's where it's at," Richard said.

As soon as Richard stepped off the chair, conversations in the room began buzzing anew. He waved his arm to Jim, motioning for him to wait.

Matt turned to Jim. "Who's that Pritchind? That name rings a bell," Matt said.

"Maybe you heard my father mention it," Jim said. "I think they know each other."

Matt looked into the distance as though trying to remember where he heard the name.

"That's it," Matt said. "The Fourth of July. The picnic supper. In the church basement. I heard your mother mention something about a Loren Pritchind, but for the life of me, I can't remember what she said. It had to be that night that I heard his name."

Richard finally made his way to Jim.

"Jim, we've received a call inquiring about you." Richard gave the message as Matt stood to the side listening.

"Who was it?" Jim asked.

"Your father," Richard answered. "He's in the city this weekend and wants to talk to you."

At the mention of his father Jim's face flushed.

"You didn't tell him where I live, did you?" Jim asked.

"I couldn't," Richard said. "I don't know your address. At any rate, your dad left his phone number and asked you to call."

Richard handed the small note with the phone number to Jim who crumpled it into a small wad in his hand without first giving it so much as a glance.

"Thanks, Richard. Thanks for the message."

Richard did not see Jim's fingers crumple the message, but Matt did.

The evening had started out well for Jim and after working all week, he had looked forward to the change of pace on Saturday evening. But the mention of his father's name caused the scowl to grow on his face and shortly after getting the message he was ready to leave The Center. Within minutes he and Matt were on their way back to their duplex.

"What's going on between you and your father?" Matt asked on the way to their apartment. "Why don't you talk with him?"

"There's nothing to be gained in talking with him. I know what happened between my mother and him. That was enough."

"That's another thing. You keep hinting that some awful thing happened between your mother and father, but you never talk about it. What happened?" Matt asked.

"It's a long story."

"So, what else is there to do?" Matt pressed. "Anyway, I think it's about time you leveled with me."

Jim opened his mouth and a low, drawn-out sigh came out.

"I told you it's a long story. Well, I'm not going to give you all the details. They're too private, anyway. You know my dad was the pastor of a church in this city when I was in high school. We lived in this city since I was born. That's how I know it so well. Here's where I'm going to make the story short. One day when I was in grade school my mother was visiting some old lady in the congregation. My mom came back to the parsonage and found three guys ransacking the place. They were looking for money, valuables – anything worth stealing. That's a howl – looking for valuables in a minister's house. I guess they thought they'd get collection money. Well, when my mom came into the house one of them assaulted and raped her. When I came in from school she was still lying on the floor. The guys who broke into our house really beat her up. She was unconscious when I came in from school."

"Did you know they raped her?"

"Naw. I was too young to really know what it all meant. I knew in a general sort of way, but all I really knew for sure was that she was all beat up and bloody and I couldn't wake her up."

"What happened then?"

"I called the police," Jim continued, "and they sent for an ambulance. They never did find the guys. Mom was hysterical when she went to the hospital. Man, she just about went nuts. She ended up in a sanitarium for a couple months. When my dad came home that day and found out about it, he never said so, but he always acted like he blamed my mother for what happened. He still does. Do you know that not once did he ever tell her that he was sorry for what happened to her! Not one time! That's why my mom took it so hard. Then, he finally accepted the preacher's job in Willow Glen. She insisted that we get away from the city. And the older my mother gets, the more it seems to bother her – the way he treats her and all. Maybe I shouldn't tell you, but what the hell. They haven't slept together since then. He gets up in sermons and tells families how they should love each other. Then, he does that. It always freaks me out when I hear him tell other people how to live. I mean, a person can belong to any church he wants and believe any creed he wants, but when that person is such a hypocrite that he hurts people in the name of religion – well, I don't know. Sometimes I really feel sorry for the people my dad counsels. He doesn't really understand sexuality at all, and I wonder how many lives he's ruined because of his ignorance."

"Why doesn't your mother leave him?" Matt asked.

"Turn the story around," Jim answered. "Why didn't you stay with Marie?"

"Huh?"

"Oh hell. If you're so goddam dumb that I have to explain it...."

"I understand. I understand, I guess," Matt stammered.

"My mother needed my dad but he wouldn't give her any support. She keeps hoping. Who knows why some people split up and others settle down to a slow death together? Hell, it's too deep for me to figure out. All I know is, sex is as basic and natural as breathing. But it sure messes up lots of lives. Preachers can't pour people into molds like candles. They're too different for that. But boy, try to tell that to my father."

"But what has that to do with your father now?"

"My father doesn't see anything gray. It's either all black or all white. Do I have to spell it out what he thinks of gay people?"

"But when you were in high school and started to act gay, didn't your parents see it then?" Matt asked.

"In high school?" Jim blurted out. "You've got to be kidding!"

"Long before that ever happened with my mother – when she was assaulted, I mean – I knew I was different than a lot of the other kids. I told you a long time ago that me and Willie Blatz were the best of friends and that we did everything together. Man, back in the eighth grade already I thought Willie was the greatest. No lie – I loved him. We felt that way about each other for a couple years before we ever had sex. I mean, we really loved each other. The sex came only after we already talked about the way we felt toward each other."

"Didn't your dad know about you and Willie?"

"Aw, he knew we were close friends. But I don't think he ever suspected we were lovers. Man, he would've gone through the roof. Me and Willie always took care to have sex when nobody, and I mean nobody else was around. We had some good times up in that choir loft. I guess you could say I was lovingly reared in the church."

"Did your dad always hate homosexuals?"

"I guess so. Ever since my mom was attacked he always mentions homosexuals and rapists in the same breath. Homosexuals and rapists. Homosexuals and rapists. He always does it."

"Some homosexuals do commit rape," Matt offered.

"And so do some heterosexuals," Jim shot back.

"Do you think your dad will ever change his attitude?"

"Who knows?" Jim said. "Now, he hates homosexuals too much. He's convinced that if any rights are given to them it will be the beginning of end of the human race. He sees organized religion as the last fortress against the total collapse of morality. He's never taken the time to see that love between many gay men is more intense and compassionate than that between many heterosexual married couples. My dad's basically scared to death of gay men. No lie, he's really afraid of them."

"While you were in high school," Matt began, "did you ever try to sit down with your dad and talk to him about... about you and Willie?"

"No. Never. Not once. He would never have understood."

Jim spoke emphatically.

His staccato answer ended their conversation.

12

During the next two weeks, spot announcements on radio and television for the candidacy of Loren Pritchind became more frequent.

When Matt came home from work on Wednesday afternoon he turned on the television and caught the end of Pritchind's political advertisements.

"For sound fiscal policy, strong leadership, and return to traditional values," the announcer was saying, "Loren Pritchind deserves your vote. Loren Pritchind is worried for your children. He doesn't want them molested. He doesn't want them kidnapped. He doesn't want your children harmed in any way. That's why a vote for Loren Pritchind is a vote against sexual deviates. Loren Pritchind is staunchly committed to protecting your children from homosexuals."

Matt changed channels. He stood back from the set for several moments as he watched the sitcom. Satisfied, he stepped away from the television to the bathroom, pulling his T-shirt over his head.

Matt had already taken off his workboots and socks, Levi's and shorts when he heard the doorbell ring, above the din of the water against the tiled shower wall.

"Damn," he muttered to himself. He reached into the stall and turned off the water; then grabbed a towel and wrapped it around himself.

His heavy footsteps vibrated as he made his way to the outside door of the duplex.

"Is Jim home?"

The visitor looked past Matt, craning his neck to get a better look inside the apartment.

"He's at work. You're Willie, aren't you? Willie Blatz?"

"That's right. How'd you remember?" Willie smiled his satisfaction at being remembered.

"Jim's not here. Doesn't get off work till eleven. Can I give him a message?"

"Uh, no. I was in the neighborhood and thought I'd stop by to see him for a couple minutes. Nothing important."

"Well, he's not here."

"You don't mind if I come inside for a minute, do you?"

Matt stepped back from the door to let Willie enter.

"Looks like I caught you at a bad time," Willie said. He pointed to Matt's bath towel.

"No problem."

There was an awkward pause before Matt continued. "Give me a minute and I'll put on some pants." He turned toward the bedroom.

"Hey, no. I don't want to interrupt your evening. I only stopped by to ask Jim if he'd be busy two weeks from this Thursday night. Eric's having a Shattersheen Party and I thought maybe Jim would want to go. Oh, you're invited, too," Willie added.

"What's a Shattersheen Party?"

"You've never been to one?" Willie asked in amazement. "Shattersheen is dishes – it looks like expensive china and crystal but it's all shatterproof, heatproof, frostproof, crackproof, and best of all, scarproof. And it's guaranteed to keep its sheen for a lifetime. I go to a Shattersheen Party at least three times a year. Great way to meet people."

"Does Jim know Eric?"

"I don't know."

"Who else will be there?"

"About fifteen of us. They'll all be gay. Doris Buckler will be the salesperson. She's a treat. About seventy years old, but she acts and moves like she's half that age. Last year Harry laughed so hard during one of Doris's parties that he fell off his chair and almost crushed her poodle. I laughed more during those four or five hours than I generally do in four weeks. Want to come?"

"Jim works every night till eleven. I don't think he could make it." Matt paused. "I don't know if I want to go alone."

"Go alone," Willie yelled, "there'll be about fifteen other guys there. And I'll be there. Alone, as a matter of fact. Me and Earl broke up."

"Oh."

Matt hesitated.

"We were together for almost two months," Willie explained. "Would you believe it. One day he just gets up and says he wants to move on. At first I thought he meant that both of us should move to another city or something like that. I started to tell him that I didn't want to quit my job and pull up stakes here. But then, out of the clear blue, he looks at me and says he wants to move on – alone. Talk about feeling sick. Wow! He started to pack and I just watched him. I kept asking him to reconsider. Give it more time. Anything, just not to walk out on me. But he wouldn't listen. After he left and I watched him pull away in his car, Matt, I went into the bathroom and got sick. But...."

Willie's voice trailed off as he glanced around the apartment.

"Hey, you don't mind if I sit here for a couple minutes and watch some television, do you?"

Willie stared at Matt's face and waited.

"You'll have to watch by yourself till I take my shower."

"Hey, don't sweat it. I don't have any plans for the evening."

Willie had already moved to the television, spinning the dial to scan each channel's offering. Matt returned to the bathroom.

The sound of the water jet in the shower stall could be heard again and Willie turned the volume higher so that it could be heard over the torrent from the bathroom.

Willie propped himself onto the sofa and kicked off his shoes so he could curl his toes behind the end cushion.

Matt wore casual slacks but no shirt when he returned to the room.

Willie glanced up for a minute before swinging his feet to the floor. He patted the cushion next to him as an invitation for Matt to sit there. Matt accepted.

"How do some of these sitcoms get on the air?" Willie said. "Look at that! They're dumb. Really dumb. Don't you think so?"

Matt grunted his agreement.

"Can you believe any wife would act so dumb?"

"I can believe it; I was married," Matt answered.

"I never knew that!"

"Four years."

"Then what did you do? Just split?"

"I guess you'd call it that."

"You know how it feels to be rejected then, don't you?" Willie asked.

"I guess so. But I'm not sure who rejected who."

"Both of us have a lot in common then, don't we? You only met Earl that first night you got into town, didn't you?"

"Your lover?"

"Yeah, Earl."

"I only met him that once."

"Since he left town I've been staying to myself. Haven't gone out much. Except to work. Tonight's the first time I've gone out at all. Socially, that is."

Willie's right hand moved to Matt's leg.

"Do you live alone?" Matt asked.

"Yeah. Now that Earl's gone."

Willie leaned his head on the back of the sofa and let his hand slide back and forth on Matt's leg.

"Do you buy a lot of Shattersheen?" Matt asked.

"Huh?" Willie took his hand off Matt's leg and looked him in the face.

"Jim and I use some crackproof stuff we bought down at the discount store," Matt said.

"Who cares?" Willie rested his head on Matt's shoulder and slowly began massaging the palm of his hand over Matt's chest.

Matt leaned his head against the back of the sofa and closed his eyes.

"Do you and Jim watch much television together?" Willie asked.

"Hardly ever. He works. I'm here alone every night."

"Maybe I should come over more often in the evening," Willie commented.

"Does Shattersheen ever crack?"

"Christ! Forget the dishes, will you?" Willie complained. With his index finger Willie began to draw slow, imaginary circles on Matt's bare chest.

"Me and Earl used to watch television a lot," Willie said.

"Addict, huh?"

"It wasn't so much the shows. I couldn't even tell you what most of them were about."

"Then why'd you watch it?"

"So we could do what we're doing now."

"Oh," Matt answered.

"I like to be close to another man. Know what I mean?"

"Yeah."

"I like to be held by another man. Know what I mean?"

"Uh-huh."

"You're sure as hell not much of a talker," Willie offered.

It was nearly eleven o'clock when Willie sat on the edge of the sofa and asked a question.

"Mind if I shower before I leave?"

"Jim'll be home soon."

"I'll be finished before he wants in the bathroom. He'll probably want a shower as soon as he gets in."

Willie got off the sofa and headed for the bathroom.

Matt got up to adjust the picture on the television when he heard footsteps on the stairs outside the door.

Jim barged into the room. "Guess who I saw?"

Matt turned and, rather disinterestedly, asked: "Who?"

"My dad. That's who."

"There's no way he can trace us here," Matt said calmly. "And even if he knows we're living in this neighborhood, how could he know which house is ours?"

"How many times do I have to tell you my dad won't give up? If he decides to do something, there's no stopping him. And he knows people all over the place. They'd help him find us," Jim said.

"And if he does find us, so what?" Matt asked. "I've had it. You're always worrying that he'll find us and you think you see him behind every shadow and shrub. I can't worry about him anymore. Maybe the time has come to stop running, sit down, and talk it out with him."

At that, Willie stepped into the room. Dried off from his shower he stood in the doorway, completely nude.

"I came over earlier this evening to see you," Willie smiled. "Wanted to ask you to go to a Shattersheen Party. Then me and Matt started to talk. Hey, are you free two weeks from Thursday evening so we...."

"It sure looks like you made yourself at home," Jim said.

Willie looked down at himself and laughed. He rubbed his fingers through his pubic hair.

"Well see, I thought I'd shower here instead of going home to an empty...."

"I don't know about the party, Willie. I'll give you a call. I've got other things on my mind that...."

The telephone rang. The three men looked at each other in silence for some moments before Jim made a move to answer it. "Yes. It's me. How did you find us?... Since you know where we live, what's the difference...."

Jim listened. Before replacing the receiver, he uttered a faint good-bye into the receiver.

"Your dad?" Matt asked.

Jim answered the question by ignoring it.

"I think maybe I picked a bad night to stop by," Willie said. He went back to the bathroom and soon appeared fully clothed.

"Give me a call when you have a chance, Jim. I really want to get together with you. All right?"

Jim nodded as Willie walked to the door.

"You too, Matt. I'd like to get together with you again," Willie said.

Willie's eyes studied Matt for several minutes before he opened the door and closed it behind him.

"I guess your dad's coming right over," Matt said when they were alone.

"As soon as he can get a taxi," Jim answered. "How long has this been going on between you and Willie?"

"Huh?"

"Don't act innocent with me, Matt."

"Willie came over to see you, Jim. Tonight's the first time he's ever been here. He came to invite you to a party then he started talking and he seemed depressed. So I tried to cheer him up, that's all."

"Did he have to take all his clothes off to get cheered up?" Jim demanded.

"Hey, look. He took a shower. That's all. There's nothing going on between us," Matt insisted.

"I'll bet."

Jim had been pacing the apartment growing more agitated as he spoke. Finally he grabbed a jacket from the hall closet and moved to the door.

"I'm not ready to talk to my dad yet. You can stay and talk to him when he comes, or you can leave too, but I've got to get away from him."

"I can't run anymore, Jim. I'm too tired. He's chased me away for the last time. Why don't you stay and see him?"

Jim's hand was poised on the doorknob as he listened to Matt. He was tempted to follow the suggestion, but he remembered what his father had said.

"My dad told me he got our address from Marie. You wrote her and gave her our address. God damn you, Matt! Why can't you keep your mouth shut! First that. Then I come home and find you with Willie."

Jim pulled the door open, then fled down the steps into the October night.

Within the past hour it had begun to rain and the persistent drizzle covered Jim's face as he ran down the street. He had no destination in mind. He was not running anywhere but away. The exertion of running, combined with the realization that his father had finally located him, caused Jim to break into a warm sweat that gradually turned to a hot and burning discomfort. His clothing grew wet with sweat and rain but he continued running till finally, in exhaustion, he slumped against a fence. Moisture was dripping off his hands. He took several deep breaths to regain his wind. After a few minutes he drew himself up from the fence and began walking. Walking at least provided the illusion of going somewhere. By now, the streets and sidewalks were slippery from the fallen leaves that clung to the wet concrete. He slipped several times. The leaves may as well have been patches of ice.

Jim was headed downtown. Fifteenth Street seemed to beckon Jim. He crossed the railroad tracks, which acted as a silent boundary to the entrance of the district, and began walking down Fifteenth Street. Under any other circumstances he would have been unwilling even to drive in this area alone. But tonight he did not care.

"Maybe," he thought, "this is where I really belong. Maybe my entire life to this moment has been a lie." The repulsion, so vivid in the past, tonight gave way to an indifference. Perhaps this was his place. Perhaps this was his life. He saw the familiar figures in the doorways and on the streetcorners, but this evening he saw them as equals, not inferiors. There was no desire to run. No urge to escape. As he waited at an intersection for the cross traffic to stop, a car pulled up beside him and the driver rolled down the window.

"Hey, buddy, want a ride?"

"Naw. I'm on my way to meet somebody."

Jim knew it was not the offer of a ride that prompted the guy to stop.

The guy got the message and although Jim hadn't anyone in the world to meet, he was too exhausted to become involved.

Jim walked past the laundromats, the dimly-lit stores and abandoned buildings amid a gallery of silhouettes. Without warning, someone stepped from a doorway and stood in his path.

"Hey! Weren't you down here a couple weeks ago?... Yeah, you and that other guy in the car. I remember. Three fuckin' bucks. You and that other queer with you tried to make a dumb ass out of me. I don't like smart-mouth queers. That's some jacket you're wearing. I need one," the kid said.

He reached over and yanked the collar of Jim's jacket.

"For the bull you and your buddy gave me a couple weeks ago, I ought to get some bucks; or maybe somethin' else."

The kid rubbed both his hands over the front of the coat.

"Oh no you don't. Get your hands off that."

Jim pulled away and began running down Fifteenth Street with the kid chasing close behind. The wet, slick sidewalks made it impossible to run fast. Not only was Jim emotionally exhausted from the events of the evening, he was physically weary from the exertion of the past several hours. He wanted more than anything else to escape that kid, but neither his body nor the weather was cooperating. The muscles in his legs stretched tight as he ran down the street. He frequently slid on patches of leaves stuck on the rain-soaked pavement. Jim couldn't lose that kid. The kid was stocky and his attitude insistent. Jim was not anxious to get into a fistfight, certainly not after all that he had already been through that evening, and he hoped the sight of a potential customer or even a cluster of loiterers on a streetcorner would discourage his pursuer.

Jim had run several blocks when the sight of two men leaving a liquor store offered the distraction he had hoped for. Seeing other people gave him a burst of energy to run the remaining distance to them.

"What's the matter, buddy? Somebody chasing you?" the one called to Jim.

"Him!"

Jim pointed back to the kid but he was so winded that no other words were possible. He leaned against the front of the abandoned house beside the liquor store. Resting his head against the bricks, he panted to catch his breath.

"Buddy, you're lucky you ran into us. That guy who's chasing you — he's a mean one." The man laughed and put Jim's arm around his shoulder to give him some support.

"Kenny's right," the other added. "You never know who you're gonna bump into down here." The second one propped himself on the other side of Jim.

At that, Jim's pursuer caught up with him and stood directly in front of the three.

"Who's this you're chasing, Paul?" Kenny asked.

Jim's eyes shot toward the one called Paul and he realized, with a shudder, that the three were friends.

"What're you gonna do with your new buddy, here?" Kenny asked Paul.

"At first, all I wanted was his jacket, but now that he's made me run so far I want more than that," he said. "Why don't we take him inside this empty house."

Jim was outnumbered and he knew it. He was pushed from behind by Paul. Each of the other two had their hands clamped on his arms, pulling him into the house. He was dragged up the wooden steps to the front porch and pushed through the open door. It had been torn from its hinges and was leaning against the wall of the front room.

Jagged fragments of glass from the shattered panes surrounded each window frame. The broken windows and the wind howling through the opening where the front door used to hang created a gush of wind stronger inside the house than on the street. Even though the wind blew through the house continuously, the plaster above the baseboards and the wooden floors reeked with the stale odor of urine and human excrement. The only illumination came from the sodium-vapor streetlights shining through the windows. Grotesquely distorted shadows danced in the room with its occupants' every movement. Jim's foot kicked against an object on the floor as he was pulled across the room. It seemed to be a mattress or cushion.

One of the strangers used his free hand to begin to pull the jacket from Jim's shoulders but he was stopped by Paul.

"Forget that jacket. I'll get it later."

Paul was clearly in charge and his orders were followed.

"Get him down on the floor."

Jim continued struggling but was no match against the three. One was standing behind him holding his arms tightly while the other one was kneeling behind him on the floor and holding his ankles in a vise-like grip. Paul stood in front of Jim and with one whipping motion unloosened Jim's belt.

"Go on, dammit. Throw him on the floor," Paul ordered.

Suddenly Jim felt his feet pulled from under him and with a thud he was pushed on his stomach to the mattress. One jumped on his shoulders while the other held his legs. Jim's squirming did nothing to free him but only served to antagonize his assailants. Without warning Jim felt a hand on the back of his head and his face was pushed down and smothered in the filthy mattress. His nose and mouth rubbed against a soggy spot in the mattress. When Jim tried to breathe he inhaled the acrid odor of urine with every gasp. His lips and tongue were pressed into the drenched and matted material. On his third breath he began to gag and choke, then finally he began to vomit.

"Aw, look what he's doin' now," the one on his shoulders complained.

"Hurry up, Paul, I don't want to get this crap all over me."

Jim had nowhere to turn his head or mouth and he was forced to taste and smell not only the mattress but also his own vomit.

"Aw man! Get a whiff of that!" one of them hollered. "Hurry it up, Paul!"

Paul remained oblivious to the comment and he was less interested in how Jim or the other two felt than in his own plans.

Jim felt the cold fingers of Paul's hand feeling his body where his Levi's had been pulled down. With every bit of his strength Jim thrashed his shoulders and legs to escape, but the weight of the three bodies on top of him was too much. The room was cool and damp, but suddenly there was no mistaking the sensation Jim felt at his neck.

"Now, buddy, you can either do it Paul's way or your way," a voice commanded. "I've got a switchblade about an inch from your neck and by God if you make another move, I'm gonna shove it right through your throat."

Jim's body went limp, as the ice-cold tip of metal touched the side of his neck just below his right ear.

"Now, that's better," Jim was advised. "Just relax now, so Paul can do what he wants. If you move one more time I'm gonna use this blade. I did it last week to another queer and I'm not afraid to do it again. And believe me, the police in this city don't worry about one dead queer."

"These fags are only good for two things," Paul said. "Getting money out of 'em, and if you can't do that, then using 'em like women when you need a good fuck. That's all they're good for, anyway."

The icy tip of the blade continued to scratch the flesh below Jim's ear as he felt his Levi's being pulled below his knees. Jim reeled with pain as he felt Paul enter his body. The thrusts of pain which shattered his body were repeated. Again and again and again. With each thrust, it seemed that the size of Paul's organ grew larger and penetrated deeper. Finally, Jim felt as though the flesh of his own body were being torn apart.

After Paul had finished, he got off Jim's body and stood beside the mattress.

"Now, that feels better."

Paul breathed heavily for several moments.

The other two made a move as though getting off Jim.

"Wait a minute," Paul ordered. "I gotta piss. Drag that queer over here. Open his mouth. I'll teach this smart-mouth queer what his mouth can be used for."

The anger Jim had initially felt upon being chased down the street had turned to panic once he was forced inside the house. It was that panic that had made his body go limp. But now, anger and panic were changing to another emotion. One that Jim had never before experienced: pure rage. For the first time in his life, Jim actually wanted to kill.

In the process of obeying Paul's orders the two loosened their grip and Jim immediately seized the opportunity. In the split second that Jim's body was not restrained, he doubled his fist, and using the energy that surged both from his rage and his desire to escape, he slammed his fist into the pit of someone's stomach. The darkness didn't let him see who got the punch nor did Jim care, but there was a muffled gasp and someone fell to the floor. Jim pulled up his pants. But immediately he felt a pair of hands around his neck. His breath was cut off. He saw the outline of someone in front of him. His neck was being crushed between the pressure of two hands. Jim steadied his right knee and with one upward snapping motion he hammered his knee directly into the groin of his attacker. The pressure around his neck suddenly released and the shadowy figure before him collapsed to the floor, screaming.

Jim did not bother with the remaining person in the room. He raced for the door. He had one thought: to escape.

He fled down the street as fast as he could run. He thought that he had finally escaped only to glance back and see one of the three still pursuing him. The rain had grown heavy and traction on the sidewalk still more difficult.

Jim came to an intersection. He dodged cars as he ran to the curb on the other side of the street. He did not see the pothole filled with water around the sewer drain. When his foot hit the puddle and fell several inches, he broke his stride. He tried to catch himself, but lost his balance. He fell to the pavement, cracking his head against the cement curb when he fell. It was only a matter of seconds before he felt hands on his neck again.

"If we weren't right here on this goddam streetcorner," his assailant hissed, "with cars passing, I'd tear your body apart with this blade."

Jim felt a circle being traced on his back. He was helpless. Fighting to remain conscious, he did not have the strength to move or to offer the least resistance. His head was thumping with pain and he was on the verge of blacking out when he felt his jacket and shirt being ripped from his back. Jim felt someone reaching into his back pocket for his wallet.

"You only got two goddam bucks in here."

Jim saw his wallet tossed on the sidewalk.

Something was suddenly slammed into his bare back.

Suddenly Jim could not breathe, the taste of blood filled his mouth.

He could not move, and he felt himself losing consciousness.

His mind seemed to be separating from his body; his body, becoming weightless.

Jim tried desperately to open his eyes.

He caught the distorted image of a large object at the curb. Flashing blue lights made him even dizzier than he had been.

Jim felt something pressed into his abdomen under his ribs. Suddenly his entire body was rolled over. He tried to focus his eyes.

Boots. Black boots. Dark uniform. Holster. Gun. Cops. Two cops.

"Call for an ambulance," one of them said. "Corner of Fifteenth and Labelle. Stabbing victim. Back wound. Looks like he's been raped, too. Pants are bloody."

"Jesus Christ," one cop said. "You'd think these fags would stay home at least on rainy nights."

"Aw hell, they don't know what it's like to stay home at night. They're like rats and cockroaches. Sleep all day. Cruise all night."

"Too bad they didn't kill him," the other cop said. "That would give us one less headache every night."

The other cop laughed.

They waited for the ambulance.

13

"Is my son here?" the preacher demanded when Matt opened the door to the duplex.

"No. But come in. Out of the rain."

The Reverend Gordan Renalski stepped into the room and removed his narrow-brimmed hat. The cloth of the hat was dark from rain and the brim did not shield the preacher's eyeglasses from the raindrops. He removed his glasses and held both his hat and spectacles in one hand while with the other, he pulled a clean, white handkerchief from his pocket to wipe the water from the spattered lenses. When this was accomplished to his satisfaction, he replaced the round, metal-framed spectacles and for the first time, looked at Matt.

"I spoke to my son not more than an hour ago on the telephone. This is where I called. Where is he?" he demanded brusquely.

"After he spoke with you, he went out. His exact words, as I recall, were: 'I'm not ready to talk to him yet.'"

The preacher squinted at Matt.

In a tone only slightly less antagonistic, the preacher asked, "Do you think he'll be back soon?"

"Probably not."

The two men stared at each other, each waiting for the other to speak. Finally, Matt gave in.

"If you want to wait, perhaps Jim will come back in a while. He didn't say how long he'd be gone."

Matt extended his hand to take the preacher's wet hat and waited as the preacher dropped the raincoat from his arms.

Matt carried the wet hat and raincoat to the kitchen and spread the coat over the back of a chair to dry. When he returned to the living room the Reverend Gordan Renalski was already sitting on the sofa. Matt sat in a chair opposite him.

The preacher cleared his throat while he gazed at Matt.

"Everything would be so much easier if you would only drop out of my son's life," the preacher began. "Let him alone. You prevented him from going to college. Will you ruin his entire life?"

These pronouncements, so easy for the preacher to utter, were difficult for Matt to address.

"I didn't make Jim come here. He chose to do it," Matt said.

"You made him do it," the preacher snapped. "I'm sure of that. Already back on your farm you enticed him. I know it. And, now look where he is. Living in a place they call the gay ghetto."

The preacher's knuckles shone white as he clenched his fists in his lap.

"Why don't you try to understand other people?" Matt said softly. "Your wife, for example. Would it be too much for you to try to understand how she felt after the assault?"

As soon as Matt asked the question he was sorry. "Forget I said that. It's really none of my business."

The preacher's eyes fixed themselves on Matt in a rigid, prolonged stare and his lips pursed tightly.

"So Jim told you about the time my wife was beaten and raped...."

The preacher's eyes continued looking in Matt's direction but Matt had the feeling that the preacher was looking less at him than into the memory of past events – painful, personal events that had left indelible scars.

"For weeks after the assault I visited my wife every day while she was at the sanitarium. She never talked. The expression on her face was one of bleak terror. I never told her that her rapist repeatedly called the house and warned me that if she ever testified against him in court, he'd kill her. The rapist had also found out that I had a son and I was warned that if I did anything to help the police, they'd do something to Jim. So, since then I've lived in fear. Fear for my wife. Fear for my son. Fear for myself. The calls stopped after a while. And my wife returned home. But before she did, the doctors told me it may be a long, long time before she recovered. I don't think she ever has."

Matt listened without answering.

"I don't mind telling you, Mr. Justin, since that happened to my wife – and may God forgive me for this – I have learned how to hate. I saw how my wife was torn apart. I've seen what it's done to our marriage. And I know how my personal life has been shattered. Hate is probably not a strong enough word to describe the feelings I have toward a person who commits such a crime."

"I didn't know," Matt answered.

"Through the years I've channeled my hate into action," the Reverend Renalski continued. "I may not do much, but I've tried to fight violence in the small ways I know how. I've tried to fight for the principles I believe in. I know some people have misinterpreted me. I'm sure Jim does."

"Jim thinks you don't understand what homosexuality is all about," Matt said.

"I've been in the ministry for a long time, Mr. Justin. I've seen many people. Counseled more couples than I can remember. I've known many people whose lives were ruined because they misused and abused their God-given sexuality. You, Mr. Justin, are a perfect example. Long ago I decided what my principles would be. I decided that sexuality is for one thing: bearing children. Any other use of sexuality is wrong. Immoral. Sinful. Evil. For that reason I feel perfectly justified in condemning anything that goes contrary to the proper use of one's God-given sexuality."

"And where does love fit into this scheme?"

"Love is an ideal, Mr. Justin. An other-worldly ideal. A fantasy that people seek but which doesn't exist here. Love is like justice. Neither is found in this world. If there were justice, the three men who beat and raped my wife would have been caught and punished. But they went completely free. No, Mr. Justin, there is neither love nor justice. This is why I must smile whenever I hear homosexuals talk about love."

The Reverend Renalski paused to look around the room. Finally, he spoke but the words came out haltingly. "I'll do all I can to get my son away from you. But even more important, I'll do all I can to fight your kind."

Determination sharpened every syllable the preacher uttered.

"Oh, I know all about you homosexuals," Reverend Renalski said. "You're all alike. You go down on Fifteenth Street every night. You're no good – none of you... and your kind never amounts to anything... look what you did to your wife. And to your son, Greg. But I'll see to it that you don't ruin your son's life. Or *my* son's life."

"Do you know where Jim works?"

"You've probably taught him to live on welfare," the preacher said.

"Or does he make his living on Fifteenth Street?"

Matt came to the edge of his chair.

"He got a job in the hospital the first week we were here."

"Probably no thanks to you," the preacher insisted. "What do you do? Stay here while he goes out every day and makes money for both of you?"

Matt jumped off his chair and was about to grab the preacher's shirt. The phone rang. Matt stood with his arms raised; the preacher remained seated while his eyes followed Matt to the phone.

"Hello... yeah, he lives here... who's calling... what did you say happened?..."

He held the receiver without saying more. Finally, he replaced it on the cradle.

"The police found Jim on Fifteenth Street. He's in the hospital now. He's been stabbed."

Matt ran to the closet and pulled his coat from a hanger. Rushing to the door of the duplex, he turned to Jim's father.

"Are you coming?" Matt shouted. "Or are you going to sit there all night?"

The preacher jumped to his feet and hurried to the kitchen for his hat and coat.

Once they arrived at the hospital the preacher did not wait for Matt, but gave his name at the receptionist's desk and asked to see his son.

"I'm sorry, sir," the receptionist said, "but that's impossible. Your son's in surgery now and the best I can do is ask you to wait. As soon as there's any word, I'll have you paged over the intercom."

Matt and the preacher walked to the waiting room, each of them taking care to sit as far as he could from the other.

Visitors rushed through the emergency entrance. Without exception, they stopped at the receptionist's desk only to be told to have a chair in the waiting room.

Shortly after Matt was seated, an ambulance pulled up at the entrance and several paramedics removed a stretcher with a young boy lying on it. The parents were with the child and the mother was crying. Matt heard the attendants refer to an accident at home.

"The police will want a statement," Matt heard one of the attendants tell the father.

Matt watched as the child was wheeled down the hallway and the parents came into the waiting room and sat down on the bench nearest the doorway. It was only minutes before two city police officers appeared and were directed by an attendant to the parents.

"What can we say?" the mother sobbed. "He went down the street to spend the night at his friend's house. He forgot something. He came running back to the house. He got some of his baseball cards. Ran out of the house. We were on the porch. Next thing we heard was the screeching of tires. We looked and saw his body lying in the street."

The woman began to sob hysterically.

The Reverend Renalski rose from his chair and spoke to the police officers. The preacher then walked over to the woman, put his arm around her shoulder, led her back to her seat.

Matt watched helplessly as the preacher quieted the woman. The Reverend Renalski held the woman's hand tightly as he comforted her. The preacher accomplished what neither the hospital personnel nor the police officers were able to do. The woman was receiving support and consolation from the Reverend Gordan Renalski.

It seemed only minutes, but when Matt glanced at the wall clock, three-quarters of an hour had passed when the two police officers finally left the room. The parents slowly walked down the corridor, and Renalski returned to his chair in the corner.

Matt overheard the parents murmur their thanks to the preacher for his help and assistance when they so needed it.

The attendants had already taken the child to surgery when two burly cops brought a young man into the hospital. The young man was unconscious and one of the cops carried him. One of the cops gave a hospital attendant a small vial for laboratory analysis. The cop suggested it might be PCP.

A limousine drove up behind the police cruiser and a nurse, dressed in starched white uniform, helped the chauffeur to ease an elderly gentleman from the back seat of his car and into a wheelchair which the nurse pushed into the hospital.

The unending parade of persons into the hospital emergency room gave Matt something to watch. The succession of persons through the entrance reminded Matt of some of the midnight movies he had watched on television back in Willow Glen. The reasons that brought these people together at the hospital were all absurd. But then, he reasoned, the accidents and tragedies of life always are. Perhaps life itself is. Without reason and beyond understanding, the emergency room seems to thrive on the fragility of human life. The longer Matt watched, the more he felt he was intruding.

Matt reached into his pocket and sorted out some change before he walked to the telephone at the far end of the waiting room. After checking the number in the telephone directory, he dialed and waited for someone to answer.

"This is Matt... yeah, Willie, I know it's the middle of the night, but I've got some bad news.... No, not about me. It's about Jim... he's in the hospital... surgery now... there's no sense in that – even if you came down here, you couldn't do anything... yeah, that's what I thought... if you could stop by on your way to work in the morning... or maybe when you get off tomorrow afternoon... he'd be happy to see you."

"Mr. Justin. Would Mr. Matt Justin please come to the receptionist's desk in the emergency room."

"Hey, Willie, I've got to run. They just paged me on the intercom. If you can't see Jim tomorrow, then maybe the next day."

Matt hung up the receiver and hurried down the hallway, the preacher following close behind. A man dressed in surgical greens awaited Matt at the receptionist's desk.

"My name's Dr. Denison. I took care of Jim. He came through surgery all right. His condition is stable. There were several problems. First, the knife wound caused a hematogenous...."

"Hey doctor," Matt interrupted. "I don't understand those big words. Just tell me in plain language. Is he going to be OK?"

Dr. Denison smiled. "Yes. He was lucky. Both the knife wound and the lacerations will heal. But he'll be in the hospital for a couple days."

"How did he get a knife wound? What happened?" The preacher's glances darted from the doctor to Matt and now that he knew his son would be all right his sole concern was with the cause of the injuries.

"I'm sure Jim will tell you," Dr. Denison answered. "Fact is, here at the hospital, we're interested in mending people, not investigating accidents." The doctor flashed a self-assured look at the preacher. "You're very lucky that your son is alive."

"Can we see Jim now?" Matt asked.

"No. He'll be in the recovery room for several hours and after he's moved to the wards he'll be groggy for several more hours." Dr. Denison looked at his watch. "It's almost 6:00 a.m. now. Why don't you wait till visiting hours this afternoon. Jim probably won't be able to talk to you till then anyway."

"Only one other question, doctor," Renalski pursued. "Did my son ask to see me when he was brought in?"

"He may have. I didn't hear it. The only name I heard him say was Matt's."

"Doctor, I've never met you before," the preacher began, "but I thank you for helping my son. I may not show it. But I wouldn't want my son to be hurt for anything. There should be more people in the world like you."

Dr. Denison smiled at the preacher.

"There are, Mr. Renalski. I assure you, there are."

Dr. Denison turned to Matt. "I was sorry when I was called to the operating room and found out it was Jim. Several weeks ago when Dr. Joe Stegler and I had dinner with you and Jim, I thought we'd warned him sufficiently about Fifteenth Street."

Matt shrugged.

Reverend Gordan Renalski watched Dr. Denison turn and walk away.

14

When Jim's eyes opened, the clock in his hospital room read 3:34 p.m. Earlier in the day he had been dimly aware of voices in the corridor and he faintly remembered doctors and nurses coming in and going out of the room. But now his eyes could make out the numbers on the clock and he was groggily aware of his surroundings.

"Ya awake now?"

Jim stretched his eyelids far apart when he heard the voice, then closed them quickly to keep out the bright glare of the afternoon sunlight. He slowly allowed the eyelids to separate again but this time he opened them ever so slowly. When they were open he looked to the foot of his bed and saw a young man about his own age studying him closely. The young man was wearing a bathrobe over his hospital gown.

"Can ya hear me?"

When the young man spoke again, Jim looked at him more carefully. His shoulder-length blond hair, cut in a Dutch-boy style, framed a friendly smile. The hospital gown, hanging loosely on his skinny frame, made him look anemic and underfed.

"Ya ain't deaf, are ya?"

Jim tried to answer the question because the remark amused him. At first his mouth was so dry that no sound came out when he tried to speak. He swallowed several times, but even this exercise didn't remove what felt like a cluster of dry marbles in his throat. The young man saw Jim's pain and he stepped to the bedstand where he poured a glass of water from the ice pitcher. Without speaking, the young man placed his right arm behind Jim's shoulders and helped him sit upright in bed; with his left nand the young man raised the glass of water to Jim's lips, allowing him to take several sips through the straw in the glass. Gently, he helped Jim lay back in bed. After several more moments, Jim answered the young man's question with one of his own.

"If I were deaf, how could I hear you?"

"Read my lips! That's what my brother does." The young man stepped to the foot of the bed and placed his hands on his hips.

"That's some slash ya got on your lip," the young man said.

As though discovering his injuries for the first time, Jim slowly raised his fingers to his mouth and felt the swollen lip.

Racing down the street. The pothole. Falling. Concrete curb. It was coming back to mind.

"My name's Harley. Harley Robbins. I'm in that bed over there." He pointed to the other bed in the room.

"I'm Jim."

"I was gettin' nervous about ya. Ya were in this bed when I woke up this morning. But jeez, ya never moved all day! I thought maybe ya was gonna die or somethin' crazy like that. Once ya groaned real loud and, hell, I went runnin' out in the hallway for a nurse. But when she came back in with me, she said ya was all right. Man, I've been standin' here all day keepin' a watch on ya. I'd get real nervous if somebody died in the same room with me."

Even the faint smile that rose to Jim's lips caused a stabbing pain to surge through his mouth and cheek. He tried again to touch his mouth but discovered that he had difficulty moving his arm. He then felt the tight bandage wound around his chest and back.

Falling. Something in his back. A fist? A knife? It slammed into his back. Someone running away. The details were fuzzy; only fleeting images flashed through his mind.

"I got shot."

Jim's mind turned from his own body to Harley's voice.

"What?" Jim mumbled.

"I said, I got shot. That's why I'm in the hospital. I was in the pool hall over on Fifteenth Street one night a while back. A fight broke out. I got shot. All I was doin' was playin' pool and all of a sudden, *bang! bang! bang!* Three shots rang out and I caught one of 'em. Doc said that if that goddam bullet'd been two inches closer to my heart, I'd be a dead duck."

"Fifteenth Street?" Jim asked.

"Yeah. I guess you don't know where it is. There's a pool hall over there. It's only a couple doors from the place where my ol' lady lives."

"You married?"

"Hell, no. When I say ol' lady, I don't mean my goddam woman. I mean my goddam mom."

"Oh."

Jim's eyes were closing slowly, weighted by drug-induced sleep that he could not fend off. The eye movement was temporarily lost on Harley.

"We lived in that goddam rathole as far back as I can remember... hey, you're not passin' out on me are ya? Good God, I hope you're not dyin' on me!"

Harley looked intently at Jim. Backing away from his bed, Harley returned to his own bed where he sat on its edge while keeping a sharp eye on Jim.

This was the position that Jim's father found them in when he entered the room. The Reverend Renalski removed his coat and quietly placed it on a hanger behind the door. As soon as Harley saw the visitor in the room wearing a preacher's collar he got off the bed and stood solemnly, as though at attention.

"Goddam! He is gonna die on me; I just know it! I'll betcha that's why they sent for a priest. To say some prayers over him, huh? God, this is givin' me the creeps."

The preacher looked over the top of his eyeglasses at Harley.

"I certainly hope he's not dying. He's my son."

"Are you lyin'? Ya mean, he's got a priest for a father? Oh, Lord!" Harley was beside himself with excitement.

"I'm not a priest," Reverend Renalski explained. "I'm a preacher. A minister. With a congregation."

Harley let a low whistle trill from his lips as a broad grin covered his face.

"You're not gonna believe me, but this is the first time in my goddam life I ever talked to a goddam preacher. I seen pictures of 'em on the television set and my ol' lady used to go to a church, but I never went with her. Anyway she stopped goin' a long time ago. Hell, now she's never sober enough on Sunday mornin' to find her way to the goddam street.... What the hell's 'a matter with me. Talkin' only 'bout myself. When the nurses ain't here I been takin' care of your boy. I giv' 'im a drink of water before."

Harley came toward Jim's father and extended his hand in greeting. The preacher shook hands, rubbed the palm of his hand on his suit coat, and took several paces away from Harley. As Harley was introducing himself to Jim's father, Matt appeared at the door.

Harley motioned to Matt with his head and asked, "Is he your son, too?"

"No." Renalski's negative was emphatic.

Matt ignored the preacher and moved directly to the side of Jim's bed where he placed his hand on Jim's forearm and rubbed it softly. The movement caused Jim's eyes to open and when he saw Matt he raised his hand toward Matt's face and gently grazed his cheek.

Harley crossed his arms and tucked his fists under his armpits as a puzzled expression crept across his face. His eyes skipped from Jim to Matt to the preacher. He backed away but kept his eyes glued on the three.

Jim lowered his arm and his eyes involuntarily closed in sleep once again.

"Are you satisfied now?" the preacher asked Matt. "I went to the police station to find out where and how they found Jim."

"What happened to Jim wasn't my fault."

"If he hadn't moved to this city, he would never have been hurt."

"He was doing all right until you showed up," Matt said.

"You're ruining his life. The same way you've already ruined the lives of your wife and son."

Matt didn't answer the preacher. The very mention of Marie and Greg reopened the wounds that he had tried so unsuccessfully to forget in recent weeks. There was no simple solution to his problems. He knew that. He had never intended to hurt Marie. The last thing he ever wanted was to leave Greg. But Reverend Renalski was only complicating matters.

As he stood contemplating his predicament Matt paid no attention to the preacher standing in front of him. It was not until Renalski suddenly thrust a small sheet of paper into his hand that Matt's eyes focused on the preacher's face.

"I suggest you call this number for an appointment," the preacher said.

Matt looked at the paper. Only a name and a telephone number was scrawled on it.

"What's this?" Matt asked.

Harley turned his head to the side to catch every word.

"Someone who can help you," Reverend Renalski said. "Loren Pritchind. I've already talked to him about you. I've set up an appointment for you to see him tomorrow morning. Ten o'clock in the Winslow Building."

"Pritchind? Help me? How?"

"Face it, Mr. Justin. You are a homosexual with a wife and child and you've seduced my eighteen-year-old son. He's now in a hospital because of you. Mr. Pritchind is a counselor. He can help you overcome these – what shall we call them? – tendencies – yes, he can help you overcome these tendencies you have, so you can return to your wife and son."

"And, what if I don't want to get over these – as you call them – tendencies? Then what?"

"Then, I'll help Marie with her divorce proceedings. But, I want you to know that if it reaches that point, I'll see to it that you are declared unfit to be a father. And I'll also see to it that you'll never – not even for an hour – have the legal right to see your son again."

The preacher stared into Matt's eyes, and almost shouted.

"Believe me, Mr. Justin. I can do it. And I will."

The preacher's raised voice disturbed Jim from his heavy slumber.

"I see you finally caught up with me," Jim said to his father.

"Rest, for now," the preacher said. "Don't try to talk."

Matt interrupted the conversation and turned to Jim. "I talked to Dr. Denison today. He says you'll only be here a couple days."

"As soon as you're released, I think you should come back to Willow Glen with me and your mother," the preacher said. "You need time to be by yourself. That will change your mind. I want you to leave this city. Anyway, Mr. Justin was telling me he's thinking about leaving the homosexual lifestyle. Weren't you, Mr. Justin?"

Jim's eyes suddenly opened wide as he looked toward his father and Matt.

"Don't go, Matt. Please, don't go away."

Jim was so drowsy that even his best efforts could not prevent his eyelids from drooping shut.

Matt stooped close to the bed, kissing Jim lightly on the cheek. Harley had been on the far side of the room during Matt's conversation with Renalski, but now he walked over to Matt and the preacher.

"I mean, I don't wanna be pushy or anythin' like that, but I just seen what ya did. Man, that's enough to blow my mind! A priest whose son has got a gay lover! Man, I'll bet the Pope don't know about that!"

The preacher's eyes rolled in exasperation. "For the last time, I'm not a priest. And my son's not gay. It's only Mr. Justin who's chosen to be a homosexual. And that's soon going to change."

"Hell, it don't matter none to me," Harley said. "I been to bed with lots of different men. When I was a goddam kid I used to hustle down on Fifteenth Street. I don't do it anymore – well, not much, anyway. Too dangerous. But, I still got a couple special guys I go to bed with."

The preacher's stare was serving as judge, jury, and executioner on Harley, but Harley ignored the indictment.

"Don't you know that's wrong?" the preacher piously intoned. "What does your father think of you?"

Harley laughed. "I ain't seen that bastard in ten years."

"What did you do?" the preacher asked. "Run away from home?"

Harley glanced at the preacher in confusion.

"Hell, no. After he got my ol' lady pregnant for the sixth time, he went off to the corner saloon to celebrate on Saturday night. When he came home he started to beat up on her and us kids like he always did, so I called the goddam cops. That bastard ran out and never did come back. My ol' lady raised us kids. I think she done a goddam good job all by herself."

"Are you in school now?" Matt asked.

"Well, not exactly," Harley admitted. "See, I kinda stopped goin' to school in the eighth grade. Well, I kinda got kicked out for boozin' it up too much. Someday I'm gonna go back and go to high school and everythin'. Someday I'm gonna go to night school, and, ya know, get my goddam diploma that way. Everybody says I got enough brains to do it. If I just once get started again. Everybody says I even got enough brains to go on to one of them technical schools. And that's just what I'm gonna do. Someday, I'll just go ahead and do it when I set my mind to it."

"How long will you be in the hospital yet?" Matt asked.

Harley's hand fumbled below the belt on his bathrobe and he tugged under his hospital gown.

"Not long, I hope. I'm gettin' horny as hell stuck in this hospital. Anyways, I gotta get back home. I'll bet those goddam brothers of mine already tore that house apart. I gotta get back and keep 'em outta trouble. Fact is, I think they're lettin' me outta here tomorrow at noon. Damn, I hope so. . . ."

"Hey preacher," Harley confided. "I know you're busy and all that stuff, but seein' that I'm gettin' outta here tomorrow mornin' and I won't be seein' ya again, would ya maybe do me a favor? Would ya take a minute or two to do some prayin' with me? I never done any prayin' before and I don't know what words to use. Hell, I don't know any of that stuff, but I'm willin' to try anythin' if it would help. See, I'm kinda desperate."

Harley tossed his head back to shake his hair out of his eyes. The ever-present smile vanished from his face as he looked at the preacher.

The preacher glanced at his wristwatch and moved to get his coat.
"I'm afraid... I'm already late for an appointment I have. You must understand how pressed I am for time."

"Oh yeah... sure... hey, that's OK. Hell, what good would one goddam little prayer do anyway... huh?" A nervous laugh came from Harley as he watched the preacher walk down the hospital corridor.

"Yes sir," Harley said to no one in particular, "someday I'm gonna go to one of them high schools and get me a diploma. Someday I'll just go ahead and do it. Everybody says I got enough brains."

As Matt left the hospital room he neither stopped nor spoke, but gently touched Harley's shoulder as he passed.

15

"Wise decision! You've made a wise decision to see me," Loren Pritchind said. "I can well understand that you don't want to lose your son."

"Reverend Renalski said that if I saw you, he wouldn't interfere in the divorce. You'll tell him I saw you, won't you?" Matt asked.

"Of course, Mr. Justin, of course I will. But Mr. Justin, it isn't all that simple. You see, we expect you to go back to your wife and your son. Return to your farm. And a normal married life. But to do that, you may need several sessions with us. We'll certainly do all we can to help you overcome your homosexual tendencies."

Their conversation was interrupted as the black telephone on the desk rang and Pritchind picked up the receiver.

"Yes, it's Loren.... Have you looked into all angles of the zoning?... There must be something wrong somewhere – no place is perfect...."

As Pritchind spoke into the telephone, Matt had his first opportunity to examine the room.

The waiting room from which he had come hardly merited the name. Three straight-backed chairs with frayed seat cushions, a single floor lamp, and a magazine rack crowded the room. The magazine rack held only four magazines, each several months old. At his feet linoleum tiles, some cracked, others missing, exposed the concrete floor below.

Stale, uncirculated air pervaded both the anteroom and inner office. It was small for a doctor's office: not more than twenty feet square. A metal desk was the largest piece of furniture in the room. Apart from the chairs in which he and Pritchind sat, the room was bare. The plaster walls, bereft of pictures, diplomas, or any other sign of professional recognition, had once been painted off-white, but were now cracked and streaked with dirt. The lone window behind Pritchind's desk was large but a smoky film of dust coated the glass, and the brick wall of an adjacent building prevented more than an illusion of light from entering the room. In addition to the door from the waiting room, there was another door on the far side of the room, a tumbler lock about a foot above its doorknob.

Matt waited for an air conditioning unit to switch on so the stale air would circulate, but in vain. The stuffy atmosphere, combined with sickeningly sweet disinfectant, was beginning to make Matt feel uncomfortable.

"Now, where were we?" Pritchind asked as he replaced the telephone receiver.

"You were saying something about several sessions," Matt offered.

"Oh yes. You see, the purpose of my sessions is to help a person recognize how abnormal it is to be a homosexual, and this can't be accomplished all in one session."

"How many sessions?"

"I can't answer that yet. We'll have to see how fast you respond."

"The only thing I'm interested in, is getting Reverend Renalski off my back so I don't lose the right to see my son."

"I understand perfectly. And, really Mr. Justin, to demonstrate faith both to me and to the Reverend Renalski, I suggest you begin your therapy as soon as possible."

"What will these sessions be like? Will we talk?"

"We won't do much of that, Mr. Justin. I don't believe in talking a person to death. I believe in action. I employ a method called conditioning. To be precise, it's called aversion conditioning. I'll train you to dislike anything about homosexuality, so that in no time at all, you'll find homosexuality as disgusting and repulsive as I do. Aversion conditioning came out quite a few years ago but I think it's still the best method around. I derive a great sense of accomplishment and satisfaction in using it. I'm only sorry that so much of my time is devoted to other community agencies. I can't counsel as many homosexuals as I'd like to. Nothing would make me happier than to see homosexuality wiped off the face of this earth."

"It won't hurt, will it?"

"Giving up bad habits is never easy, Mr. Justin. But remember your

son. You do want to have the privilege of seeing him regularly, don't you?"
    Matt said nothing.
    "Shall we begin?"
    Matt nodded.
    "Fine. Fine. Follow me. It's always gratifying to help someone lead a happier life."
    Loren Pritchind stepped from behind his desk and walked to the door with the tumbler lock on it. He motioned for Matt to follow. Pritchind stood to the side as Matt entered the room.
    The floor level of the room dropped some four inches below Pritchind's office and Matt, not expecting the slight step, stumbled as he entered the room. The smooth-plastered, green-painted ceiling was broken only by a single light bulb in the center of the room. It provided some light but was not of high intensity. If the room seemed bright, it was only because all four walls were covered with white ceramic tile, some cracked and broken. The concrete floor was painted battleship gray. The room looked like a high school shower room, but without any showerheads protruding from the walls. A large drain, maybe twelve inches in diameter was directly in the center of the room under the single light bulb. A home movie screen about four feet square was mounted on the wall to Matt's left, while to his right stood a single chair. It resembled a piece of lawn furniture – all white and metal; uncomfortable looking, certainly not designed for comfort. Behind and to the left of the chair was a small table, perhaps two feet square. A stationary tub, of the kind found in any laundry room, sat in a far corner. A garden hose was attached to its faucet. The only other piece of furniture, a metal cabinet, stood in another corner.
    "Now, Mr. Justin, since this is our first session, it probably won't last long, but you'll be more comfortable if you change clothes. We don't want your clothes soiled. And, we certainly want you to be as comfortable as possible. There's a robe in that locker – you can put your clothes in there, too. Just come to the door when you're ready."
    Before he could say anything, Matt saw the door close behind Pritchind, leaving him alone in the dank, ill-lit room. He walked to the locker and opened the cold metal door. Inside was a single gown. He pulled it out and held it up. It looked like a standard hospital gown, but it didn't tie in the back. It didn't tie anywhere. It was a plain white robe, short-sleeved and completely open in front. No ties. No buttons. No zip-

per. Nothing. Just an open smock-like robe. Matt walked to the door and opened it.

"How do I tie this thing on? Do you have another one?"

"Don't worry about that, Mr. Justin. Just slip into it – the open part in front. And, by the way, take your shoes and socks off, too. Put them in the locker along with your clothes."

"What's going on here?" Matt protested. "What kind of therapy...."

Loren Pritchind interrupted. "Mr. Justin, let's get something straight. Either you cooperate here, or I'll inform Reverend Renalski. If I do the latter, you know as well as I, you may have serious difficulty ever seeing your son again."

Matt hesitated at the door, then slowly closed it.

Matt began to undress and placed his clothes, article by article, into the locker. He sat on the edge of the metal chair to pull his socks off, then tossed them into the locker. He closed the door on his clothes and went to the office door to call Pritchind, pulling the robe together modestly as he stood at the door.

"I'm ready," Matt called out.

Loren Pritchind entered the room and closed the door.

"Sit down, Mr. Justin. And get comfortable. Do you like movies?"

"They're all right. I'm not crazy about them, but... why?"

"Some therapists use still photographs. But movies work faster. We'll begin by showing you a short movie. It'll only last about ten minutes."

"How's that going to help me?"

"You'll see."

Pritchind stepped back into his office and returned carrying a small movie projector with the reel already in it. He pulled down the screen and placed the projector on the small table behind Matt's chair.

The light in the room went off and the steady whir of the projector started. In seconds, the pictures of several young men appeared on the screen. Matt was temporarily distracted when Loren Pritchind stood beside him. Pritchind was reaching down to separate the robe where Matt had drawn it about himself.

"What're you doing?" Matt demanded.

"It's necesary for me to see how you respond to this movie. I must see how long it takes your penis to erect."

Loren Pritchind's mood changed drastically. He roughly shoved Matt's arms on the metal armrests of the chair. The flickering pictures on the screen did not provide a constant illumination in the room, but there was enough light that Matt could easily see Pritchind's face. And Pritchind also could watch Matt easily.

"Now, don't think about me," Pritchind ordered. "Watch the screen."

Matt tried to concentrate on the movie. The first several minutes showed the group of young men walking down a country road. Then they left the road to walk back into a woods. Matt watched the pictures disinterestedly. There was really nothing to them.

But then, the movie zeroed in on two young men. They embraced and slowly began to undress each other. Then they began fondling each other's sexual organs.

Suddenly, the light in the room was turned on and Pritchind was standing immediately in front of Matt.

"I see you become aroused very quickly," Pritchind said. "Your homosexual tendencies must be extremely strong. I think now we can begin our therapy in earnest. Would you like to see this movie again from the beginning? This time I'll let you watch it until the end. All right?"

"If this is all the therapy involves, sure. It's not as unpleasant as I expected."

"It will be a little different this time. Now, as soon as you become aroused, I'll give you something to alter your reaction a little. This way you'll gradually learn to associate unpleasant reactions with your homosexual feelings."

"I don't know if I want anything unpleasant..." Matt began.

"You do want to see your son again, don't you?" Pritchind asked.

Matt looked at the man, then gradually settled back into the chair.

"Now, before we begin, I'll offer a suggestion," Loren said. "As soon as you begin to have an erection, I'll give you an injection of this apomorphine."

Loren held a hypodermic syringe in his hand and showed it to Matt.

"It will produce an unpleasant sensation," Loren continued. "If you want to avoid all unpleasantness, just avoid having an erection. If you don't have any, and the movie comes to an end, you get dressed and that will be the end of the session until your next appointment. It will be to your advantage to avoid becoming aroused.

"Ready?" Pritchind asked.

Without waiting for an answer Pritchind extinguished the ceiling light and started the projector again.

Matt closed his eyes.

Suddenly Pritchind stopped the projector.

"Mr. Justin, don't play games. You are to watch the movie and when necessary, I will begin treatment. Remember, you voluntarily came to see me and I'm trying to help you."

Matt's eyes opened and he watched the pictures on the screen. He tried to keep his eyes on the pictures while simultaneously forcing himself to think of anything other than what he saw before him. But the pictures were too inviting to ignore. For one thing, the one young man on the screen looked something like Jim. All Matt could think about were the many times in the past that he and Jim had been together. Much as he wanted to avoid it, he felt his body tensing. The change was not lost on Pritchind.

Suddenly there was loud banging on the outer office door.

"Now what!" Pritchind complained loudly.

"Anybody in there? Open up! I'm coming in!"

The door to the office was flung open and Willie Blatz stood in the doorway.

"Who are you?" Pritchind demanded. "What are you doing in my office?"

"Come on, Matt. Let's get out of here," Wilie said.

Matt was out of the metal chair, looking bewildered amid the confusion Willie had caused.

"Are you crazy?" Matt hollered at Willie. "Barging in here like that."

Willie opened the metal locker and pulled out Matt's clothes, tossing them in his direction.

In the confusion, Loren Pritchind laid the hypodermic syringe on the table. Pritchind tried to push Willie out the door, but Willie's strength exceeded Pritchind's. The older man threw a wild punch toward Willie's face but missed. Willie jabbed Pritchind on the right cheek and the blow sent him reeling into the metal chair.

Willie lunged toward the table and picked up the syringe.

"Do you know what's in here?" Willie asked.

"Apomorphine. That's what Pritchind told me."

"That's what I thought," Willie yelled. "Do you know what apomorphine does?"

"No," Matt answered.

"Take a good look then. 'Cause this is what Pritchind was going to give you."

Willie stabbed the hypodermic syringe into Pritchind. The man sat, dazed, in the metal chair.

Within seconds Pritchind began to groan. The apomorphine was already producing stomach cramps. Within moments, Pritchind became violently ill and began to vomit convulsively. He fell off the chair, clutching his stomach as he writhed on the floor.

"Let's get out of here," Willie said.

"How about him?"

"This is the kind of therapy he's given to gay men through the years. Let him see how it feels."

Matt ran after Willie from the room. He turned once to see Pritchind, curled into a ball on the floor, retching and screaming with pain.

The odor of vomit filled Matt's nostrils as he and Wilie ran from the office and hurried through the narrow corridor and down the two flights of steps to the ground floor. Neither said anything till they were out on the street.

"I hope you're satisfied now," Matt said angrily. "I was supposed to see him in order to work things out with my wife and son."

"Aw, come on, Matt. Grow up. Pritchind's not going to help you with your wife or son. Do you think apomorphine's going to help you get over your feelings? If you do, you're even more of a babe-in-the-woods than I thought."

"Well, that's what he said," Matt protested.

"Someday I hope we go to New York together. They've got a nice bridge there I'd like to sell you," Willie said as he shook his head.

Willie led Matt down the street two blocks before Willie pointed to a small foreign car.

"I'll drive you over to my place for some dinner."

"How'd you know I was at Pritchind's in the first place?"

"I stopped by to see Jim but he was groggy yet and kept falling asleep. But that other kid in the room talked to me a lot. He was all excited because he was being released from the hospital at noon. Kept talking about Jim's dad being a priest. I didn't know what he meant by that. But then the kid said that last night he heard the priest tell you that you should see Loren Pritchind this morning. The kid was sharp on the details. He told me your appointment was at ten o'clock in the Winslow Building. I didn't wait to talk to Jim. I took off right away for the Winslow Building."

"How did you know about Pritchind?"

"Anybody who's gay in this city knows about Pritchind. He says he's a counselor and a therapist, but in reality, he's ruined the lives of countless gay men. There ought to be a law against that kind of therapy. He's no therapist. He's a murderer."

Willie unlocked the car door and Matt got in.

"So why did you bother to get involved?" Matt asked.

Willie turned the ignition key.

"'Cause I know about Pritchind's reputation. And I didn't want to see you get hurt. And I knew you would."

The bright red car pulled out of its parking space and sped down the street.

16

It was past four in the afternoon when Richard looked at the clock in Jim's hospital room.

"Are you sure Matt wasn't at the apartment?" Jim asked.

"Not when I stopped by yesterday afternoon," Richard replied.

"When was the last time you saw him?"

"The day after I came into the hospital. Day before yesterday."

"Hasn't he called since then?" Richard asked.

"No. The other night my dad said something about him leaving the gay community. I was so groggy I can't remember exactly what was said. Could you call the apartment now and see if he's there yet?"

Richard went to the phone beside Jim's bed and dialed the numbers Jim dictated. As he waited for Matt to answer, he looked around the hospital room.

"At least you have the room all to yourself," Richard said.

"There was another guy here but they released him yesterday. I'm afraid I wasn't much company for him. I kept falling asleep. I don't even know his name. Aw, what's the difference anyway? He probably wouldn't turn a finger to help me. I'm beginning to believe everybody and everything in this world is rotten."

Richard let the phone ring a dozen times as Jim talked but there was no answer. At length he hung up.

"He's all right, I'm sure," Richard reassured Jim. "Busy, probably; and no reason to stay at the apartment for long periods of time."

Jim didn't answer as he lay in bed.

"Anything going on down at The Center lately?" Jim asked.

"Making plans for the Halloween Masquerade Party. That keeps me busy. Then, there's a group who's trying to give us a hard time about zoning. But that's nothing new. Think you'll be up and around in time for the Halloween Party?"

Their conversation stopped when Dr. Denison came into the room.

"What are you doing in bed? You should be up walking around the corridors. Getting exercise," he scolded.

Jim screwed up his nose in answer to the doctor's suggestion.

"I've got good news. I checked your charts and if all goes well, you should be out of here within the week – provided you get up and start walking around," Dr. Denison ordered.

Jim's face lit up.

"You haven't seen Matt lately, have you?" Jim asked.

"No, but I will in a few minutes. He called this morning and asked if I could talk with the two of you this afternoon at 4:30."

At this, Jim sat upright in bed and his face broke into a broad grin. "I was starting to worry that he'd left town."

In his excitement Jim anxiously watched the wall clock; it was 4:27 when Matt walked into the hospital room.

"I missed you yesterday," Jim said. "Willie stopped by in the morning but I kept falling asleep."

"I went to see Loren Pritchind," Matt answered.

"I hope it was a social visit," said Dr. Denison, "and not an appointment for one of his therapy sessions."

"It wasn't social," Matt admitted.

"Oh boy," Dr. Denison sighed.

"What's the matter?" Jim asked. "What do you mean – oh boy?"

Dr. Denison folded his arms on his chest. "Loren Pritchind has one of the worst reputations in the city for his dealings with gay people. He employs a method called Negative Reinforcement Therapy to 'treat' us. And I use the word 'treat' with sarcasm. Back in the 1940s and 1950s some people thought that if gay people would learn to associate painful reactions with homosexual attractions, they would eventually give up their gay lifestyles. Well, apomorphine is a powerful emetic."

"What's an emetic?" Jim asked.

"It's a substance which, when injected into the body, causes the brain to send strong signals to the stomach. The stomach reacts violently by expelling all contents and the person becomes deathly ill. Due to each person's reactions to apomorphine it's extremely difficult to give controlled amounts to someone; it can easily cause a person to go into convulsions and suffer cardiac arrest. Pritchind enjoys giving overdoses."

"Cardiac arrest. What do you mean by that?" Matt asked.

"Injections of apomorphine have been known to kill people. It's happened to some gay patients as a result of this therapy."

"You mean to tell me that gay persons have actually died because doctors subjected them to this kind of treatment?" Matt asked.

"Yes and no. Reputable therapists don't use Negative Reinforcement Therapy. They know it doesn't do anything except ruin lives. But this Pritchind's a quack. He doesn't specialize in counseling; he specializes in medical torture," Dr. Denison said.

"We got back at him, though," Matt said.

"How's that?"

"Well, it all happened so fast. Willie knew I was there – that Harley kid told him – so he came charging into the office like a wounded bull elephant. There was a scuffle and Willie stuck the needle into Pritchind. He was lying on the floor when we left."

Dr. Denison closed his eyes.

"It couldn't happen to a more deserving individual," Dr. Denison began, "but let's hope Pritchind doesn't win the election in November. If he does he'll crucify gay people."

Richard had listened to Matt's story in silence but now he asked, "What made you go to see Pritchind in the first place?"

"I was worried that if I didn't go, Reverend Renalski would see that I'd lose Greg."

"Good Lord, Matt, if you want to see a reputable counselor for any reason why didn't you ask me for some names. Plenty of trustworthy therapists are around – both gay and straight. I could recommend some people," Dr. Denison insisted.

"There were just so many questions popping up, I didn't know where to start answering them," Matt said.

"Such as?"

"Marie. And Greg. And leaving them. And what happened to Jim. And whether I should stay here or go back to the farm. I mean, there were questions hitting me from every side."

"That's not your basic problem," Denison countered.

"What is?" Matt asked.

"Can't you see it?" the doctor pressed.

"Don't make me play guessing games. I've already been through enough."

"Okay, Matt," said Denison. "I'll give you a couple clues. Are you really gay, or have you only reacted that way the last couple months? And do you respond only to other people's attempts to hurt you? Do you only react? Don't you ever take the initiative to better your own life? Is your life one of action or reaction?"

"What's all that supposed to mean?" Matt shot back.

"Why did you leave your wife and son in the first place?"

Matt got out of his chair and walked to the window. He looked out over the city toward the highway from which he had first entered the city. Matt turned from the window and looked at Dr. Denison.

"I realized it was a mistake for me to be married. I couldn't give Marie the affection she needed; and she sure never gave me the kind I needed. It wasn't until I met Jim that I knew what I needed and wanted.

"I hope it never happens," Matt continued, "But even if something splits me and Jim apart, I know I could never be satisfied with Marie again. I couldn't be satisfied with any woman. I respect Marie and wish her the best with anything she does, but she can't give me what I'm looking for."

"And," Denison pursued, "where does Greg fit into all of this?"

"That's the problem. Greg's something special. No matter what I am now or in the future, I'm his father. And I don't want it to be in name only. I want to do all the things a father should do for his son. I guess what I'm saying is... I don't want to lose Greg...."

"So you want to leave Marie. But you don't want to leave Greg. Is that right?"

Matt agreed.

"Would you want to return to Marie under any conditions?" Dr. Denison asked.

"No."

"Why?"

"Because we didn't get along."

"Why?" Dr. Denison insisted.

"Because... because I'd rather be around Jim."

"Why?"

"Because... because I like him."

"Why?"

"God, what do you want me to say?"

"Why did you leave Marie for Jim?" pressed the doctor.

"You want me to say it? OK. I'll say it. I'm gay. Do you hear me? I'm gay!"

"That's what you had to admit to yourself," Dr. Denison said quietly. "That's the first step in taking charge of your own life. Now that you've stated that much, what are you going to do about your son?"

"I don't know."

"Don't you care about him?"

"Of course I do."

"Then what are you going to do? Watch your wife and Renalski do what they want with him?"

"No."

"Then what are you going to do?"

"Dammit, I'll fight for my son."

"Good," Dr. Denison said as he raised his eyebrows to Jim and Richard. "Now we're getting somewhere. I wonder why people have to get angry before they'll act."

Dr. Denison looked at his wristwatch and pointed with his finger. "Matt, I've got a staff meeting in two minutes.... Next time I see you I want to hear your plans. How you're going to fight for your son.... Okay?... I know several attorneys, if you need some names."

Richard left with Dr. Denison; only now were Matt and Jim alone together.

The clanging of the meal trays on the carts in the hallways grew louder and provided a distraction for both Jim and Matt. They said nothing until the nurse's aide brought Jim's supper.

"You need any help with this food?" the aide asked Jim.

"Naw. I can manage."

"You got roast beef there. You sure you don't need help cutting it?" the aide insisted. "I had some in the cafeteria earlier and it is T-O-U-G-H," she laughed.

"No thanks. I can handle it."

The aide pushed the table over Jim's lap so he could sit upright in bed and begin eating.

As he reached for the knife and fork to cut the piece of meat, a wince crinkled his forehead. He jerked his left hand to his right shoulder.

"My right arm and shoulder's so sore I can hardly lift it yet. And this bandage sure doesn't help anything."

He tried again to cut his roast beef. The knife dropped from his fingers, clanging against the metal tray.

Matt jumped up and took the knife and fork from the tray.

"Here. Give me that."

Matt began cutting the meat into small bite-sized pieces while Jim lay back and watched. Matt took the fork and placed a small amount of mashed potatoes on it. Matt raised it to Jim's mouth.

Jim allowed Matt to choose the potatoes or asparagus or meat or salad, as he wished, and ate whatever Matt offered on the fork. Jim ate in silence, then held up his hand to signal that he didn't want any more.

"Jim... earlier when Dr. Denison and Richard were in the room, I did all the talking. You never said whether you wanted to go back to the apartment with me. You really didn't say anything. And I appreciate that. But now they're gone and we're alone. I'd like to know what you really want to do when you leave the hospital. A lot has happened the last couple months. And even more, the last couple days. Maybe you'd really like to go back with your mom and dad. Or, just move on, and start life over by yourself somewhere. If you would, I'd understand."

Jim said nothing. He closed his eyes and rested his head on the pillow.

Finally, he reached over to Matt's hand and gently touched the third finger with its simple, gold wedding band.

"I'm glad Willie helped you out," Jim said.

He passed his fingers back and forth ever so gently across the back of Matt's hand.

"Willie's probably the best friend I ever had."

"Are you trying to tell me something?" Matt asked.

"I guess really, I mean, there are two things I'm trying to say," Jim continued.

"What?"

"First, that Willie and I have been through a lot together. And he's really my best friend."

"And second? What's the second thing?"

"Remember that first day I met you," Jim started. "We were back at your farm. I tried this ring on and you told me that you didn't want me trying it on. Remember? I had to laugh to myself because you acted so dumb."

A slight grin slipped across Matt's face.

"Do you still feel that way?" Jim asked. "I mean – about my wearing your ring? Willie's my best friend, but... you're even more special to me."

Jim again touched the wedding band on Matt's finger.

Matt looked at the ring. He removed it and, as Jim held his hand forward, Matt slowly pushed the plain gold band onto Jim's finger.

"Any other questions?" asked Jim.

Matt smiled and asked no more.

17

The dry, warm days of Indian summer refused to yield to the damp chill of autumn. By the last week of October the chrysanthemums were fading and the gold and crimson leaves were falling from the trees. But the daylight hours were still warm, unseasonably so for this time of year. The clear blue afternoon skies seemed more a harbinger of spring than of winter.

Apart from one evening of rain in the city the October weather was tinderbox dry. Grass fires flared in open areas around the city as the fire marshal's ban on the burning of leaves and trash went unheeded. Lack of rainfall had shriveled the lawns and gardens long ago so that the only lingering trace of summer were the warm sun-drenched days.

It was on such an afternoon that Richard came from The Center to visit Jim after his return from the hospital.

"I'll be back to work next week," Jim was saying.

"Isn't that rushing it?"

"Dr. Denison said it was okay."

Jim rose and pulled up his T-shirt so that Richard could inspect the wound.

"See? It's almost healed."

Jim pulled his shirt back down and resumed his seat.

"Has your father stopped by lately?" Richard asked.

"Let's see. I've lost all track of time lately." Jim narrowed one eye slightly and, tracing his index finger across the invisible sheet of an imaginary calendar, tried to jog his memory. "He was at the hospital the first day I was there. Then I guess he went back to Willow Glen. He stopped by the hospital that weekend once, but only for a couple minutes. That's the last I saw him. He hasn't come here to the apartment since I've been out of the hospital. But wait – I received a strange call from him the other day," Jim continued. "It was long-distance from Willow Glen. He asked how I was feeling. Then he asked me if I was coming back home to Willow Glen. I told him no. It's funny, but he didn't seem too bothered by that. Almost resigned to it. Then he said something really weird."

"What was that?" asked Richard.

"He wanted to know if I was going to the Masquerade Ball on Halloween."

"What did you tell him?"

"I told him yes," Jim said. "It was funny. He encouraged me to go. He asked the question so fast, I didn't think to ask how he knew about it. I got the impression he wanted both me and Matt to go to the Halloween Party. Matter of fact, he said I should go and have a good time. That it would get my mind off the hospital stay. Either he's had a change of heart or he's plotting something devious. Maybe he's going to have the cops pick us up that night!" Jim laughed at his own cynicism.

Richard's concern was reflected by his worried expression.

"You say you haven't seen him since you were released from the hospital?" he repeated.

"No. Why do you ask?"

"There's a small group of people who have been visiting the mayor's office. They've also been talking to the city commissioners. Trying to close down The Center. The excuse they're using is zoning ordinances. I was tipped off about one of their meetings and I saw the group entering the mayor's office."

"So," Jim began, "what has that to do with my father?"

"I knew most of the people in the group. Loren Pritchind was there. I'd seen some of the rest at other meetings. One of those I didn't know was a clergyman. If he wasn't a minister, he was wearing a black collar...."

Jim turned to Richard.

"You think it was my father?"

"I can't be sure. But from Matt's description, I think it may have been."

"That figures," Jim said. "He won't be satisfied till he gets me and Matt apart. He'll go to any lengths to do it."

"Could you talk with him?" Richard asked.

Jim fell back into his chair, laughing bitterly.

"*Talk* to him!" Jim repeated. "What's the use? Both times he was at the hospital, I tried to do that. But he wouldn't listen. He's got tunnel-vision. Once he gets on his white horse, there's no stopping his crusades. It's impossible to reason with him – I should know. I saw my mother try to do it enough times."

"But," Richard insisted, "he's a minister; he should have a special gift for listening to people. Certainly he'd listen to you."

"You don't understand my dad. The only special sense he has is for thinking he's always right."

"There are some other ministers in the city," Richard said. "We've set up a dialogue with some of them. Would it help, do you think, if your father talked with them?"

"They'd be wasting their time. Once he gets his mind set, there's no changing it. When it comes to gay people, he's just got a blind spot."

"Any ideas?" Richard finally asked in desperation.

"Get a lawyer," Jim suggested, "to fight any zoning changes."

Richard sighed. "You're not very encouraging."

Jim rose with a shrug of his shoulders and got out of his chair.

"Plans moving ahead all right for the Masquerade Party?" Jim asked.

"No problems. I thought we might have some trouble renting the hall. But I talked to the owner and come to find out, his favorite brother is gay. So no sweat."

Jim walked to the window and, drawing back the curtain, looked down to the street. "Matt's generally home by now," he worried aloud.

"You don't really think there will be any trouble here, do you?" Jim asked, turning back to Richard. "I mean from that group my dad's joined up with? *If* it was my dad."

Richard's brow was furrowed. "Who knows for sure? I'd like to look on the positive side, but I know that some members of that group are hotheads. We've provided psychological findings, historical data, even theological opinions. We've given them correct factual information till it's coming out of their ears. But basically it's not an informational gap; it's an emotional hatred and fear. How do you deal with that?"

"Really, though," Jim mused, "really... what could happen? Good, he just drove up."

The curtain swung back into place as Jim turned from the window. Matt's footsteps could be heard bouncing up the stairs and then the door rattled open.

Matt had thrown his arms around Jim and kissed him before he noticed their visitor.

"Now that you're in safe hands, I'll leave," Richard joked.

"No need to rush," urged Matt. "Stay as long as you like."

"We were just talking about Jim's father," Richard explained.

"Oh, him." Matt turned sideways and continued through the room. Richard rose to leave.

"Will both of you be at the Masquerade Party?" he asked at the door.

"Wouldn't miss it!" Matt boomed. "Haven't decided on our costumes yet, but it should be the event of the year."

Richard raised his hand in a wave. "See you on Wednesday evening then."

Their friend gone, Jim pointed to the kitchen table.

"Got two letters today. One for you and one for me. My mom answered the letter I wrote her last week. Your letter is on the table. Looks important."

With a glance at the return address, Matt slid his finger under the sealed flap and pulled the single sheet of paper from its envelope.

> Matt,
>
> I've got myself a lawyer and begun the divorce.
>
> My father and brothers took in the crops. They're still angry.
>
> I don't know what will happen to the farm. Sell it, I guess. Maybe the lawyers will tell us. I've also heard from yours already. He's snotty.
>
> Marie
>
> P.S. I deposit the checks you send **every** other week into a special account. I don't know what you're trying to prove.

Matt read the letter a second time, then handed it to Jim.

"I guess that's that," Jim said, refolding the sheet of paper into its envelope.

"She didn't say a thing about what's most important," Matt murmured. "She didn't say one word about Greg. That's just like her."

"Do you blame it on me?" Jim blurted in his characteristic honesty. "The divorce and all?"

Matt picked up the letter and ground it into his pocket.

"Blame isn't the right word," he said. "You happened to be the person who was there when I discovered why I never felt right being married. But blame? No, that's not the right word at all."

18

The Reverend Gordan Renalski hurried through the corridor of the Winslow Building.

"Gordan, you're the last to arrive," said Pritchind, opening the door. The three chairs from the waiting room had been added to the two already in the inner office. Their occupants, all men, wore ordinary business dress and were of an appearance such as might be found anywhere in the United States. Their conversation was similarly unremarkable. Neither offensive nor edifying, their amiable banter might have been overheard in any group of middle-aged American businessmen.

"I heard a good one from my archbishop last time I spoke with him. It was the custom in this monastery that once a year, at Christmas, one monk would be allowed to break his vow of silence to say one thing he considered important. Well, one Christmas this monk stands up and says, 'I think the mashed potatoes here are too lumpy.' The next Christmas another monk gets up and says, 'Well, I *don't* think the mashed potatoes are lumpy.'"

Several men laughed.

The priest continued.

"Well, the Christmas after that, a third one steps forward and says, 'I'm getting sick and tired of you monks. All you do is complain.'"

Gales of laughter greeting the end of his joke, the priest sat back, a satisfied grin on his broad face.

"If Father Schneider is finished, perhaps we should start with our meeting," Renalski suggested, unsmiling. "It shouldn't take long."

Murmurs of assent faded to attentive silence.

"I've just come from seeing the mayor and the news isn't good," the preacher said. "Little can be done about closing that gay center for any zoning reason. The mayor says they're observing all legal regulations and there are no zoning violations."

"That's too bad," one of the others said, shaking his head. "I had hoped we could attack the problem that way."

"There's really only one way," another put in. "We'll have to get Loren elected to the city council. Only when we have a strong voice like his on that council will we be able to pass and enforce strict legislation. And voting him in should be no problem. Homosexuality has always been an emotional issue. It's easy to get voters stirred up over that. Easiest way to drive the homosexuals back into their closets."

"I still say we're using the wrong approach," said a man near the window. "Legal battles won't scare anybody. On top of everything else, they're expensive. It's a whole lot cheaper to use scare tactics. Take an animal, for instance. If you scare it bad enough, it'll cower back into a corner or else it'll run away and hide. That's all we have to do. Scare 'em. They'll run in every direction like a bunch of jackrabbits."

"Trying to scare them a little bit won't hurt anything at all," echoed another. "And it's fun."

"I have to agree. It'll quiet them down. And once they're scattered, we'll be in a better position to fight them legislatively," said the Reverend Renalski.

"When I am elected next month, then maybe we can get something done. Drive them out of the city once and for all. But we need something dramatic right now – *before* the elections," Loren Pritchind added.

From the corner of the room a man who had not spoken cleared his throat and all eyes turned to him.

"Gentlemen – and I'm beginning to have some reservations when I use that term – I simply cannot sit here and listen to what is being suggested," he began. "Several months ago when you contacted me, I was given the distinct impression I was joining a political action group to work for good government. That's fine. I'm all for that. I'll help any way I can to attain that goal. But so far we haven't had one meeting when the talk didn't eventually turn to vigilante methods. There's no way I can justify in my own mind some of the suggestions I've heard today. Scare tactics, chasing people like animals, the threatened use of force – these are all contrary to the basic ministry I've worked in all my life. I cannot condone any program that even hints at the use of violence."

The speaker's neighbor nodded his head in agreement.

"Hold on! Wait a minute!" Renalski interrupted. "Certainly I'm against violence one hundred percent. But violence and fear are two different things. Let me ask a question. Has any of us here ever delivered a sermon on the fires of hell and the torments of the damned?"

There was a general shrug of admission.

"Let us consider those sermons," the Reverend Renalski continued. "Were they violent? Did they incite your parishioners to violence? Or did they rather instill the fear of God into the soul of each one present? Is it not this very fear that leads the woeful sinner by the waters of repentance? Would it not be a wonder of the Almighty if we His servants might use this blessed fear that all homosexuals be made to repent?"

Lulled by the preacher's grandiloquence, the clergymen sat in rapt attention. The object achieved, Renalski returned to his former approach. "One of the fastest ways of getting those homosexuals back into their closets is by scaring them. Intimidation. Scare tactics, if you will. They'll work. I guarantee you. Scare them about losing their jobs. Housing. Police harassment. Believe me, it'll work."

"One question, Gordan," interjected a man who had not yet spoken. "I think you'll agree with me that there's a fine line separating fear tactics and outright violence. How do you tread that line without actually crossing it?"

"You don't mean to suggest that I'm urging violence, do you?" Renalski demanded. "I can't control what other people do. As long as I'm not advocating violence, can I be responsible for what others do? Let me assure you I wash my hands of any plan using violence."

"But what if a situation turns violent? Then what?" another insisted.

"All I can do is reiterate my opposition to violence."

"If I might have the floor for a few minutes." The black-suited priest sat forward in his chair, gazing at his colleague. "As you know, I'm here in a semi-official capacity. My archbishop wants me to report to him on the workings of this group and certainly, both he and I are grateful that you should seek our participation. But let me, in all candor, express to you some of the concerns of my archbishop. As some of you may know, our Holy Father in Rome is in the process of drawing up a list of future cardinals. The Holy Father has told my archbishop that his chances of being named a cardinal are excellent. But – and here's the big condition – *but* the Holy Father said my archbishop must take care not to cause any political ripples until he is named a cardinal and prince of the church."

"We aren't asking for any political ripples," one of the others scoffed.

"Well, you see, it's not that simple," the priest continued. "My archbishop has gone as far as he can in opposing gay people in this archdiocese. He's spoken out against their lifestyle. He's openly censured that priest over at the Church of the Good Shepherd who has ministered to queers. And he's steadfastly refused to allow the archdiocesan newspaper to print any mention of pastoral programs for queers. It may interest you to know that my archbishop has – off the record, of course – directly told the editors of the archdiocesan newspaper to print only negative and inflammatory articles about homosexuals. So, you see, my archbishop is squarely on your side. But, if he is to get that cardinal's hat in Rome, he can't dare to do anything that would link his name with this group."

"Any other comments?" Reverend Renalski asked, looking round the room.

One man leaned forward. "There's another element. Churches can't ignore the financial implications of the gay issue. The chancellor of our church told me – in strictest confidence, of course – that the gay issue is not a moral issue but an economic one. If our church supported gay rights, a few wealthy contributors would discontinue their sizable donations to the church. And smaller contributors would either reduce or discontinue their offerings. Our church leaders are crafty and shrewd when it comes to money matters. That's one of the major reasons our church opposes gay rights."

"It works the other way, too," someone else added. "If a congregation hears a preacher give a hellfire-and-brimstone sermon about queers molesting children, the donations will immediately skyrocket. The best way to get the money rolling in, is for a preacher to tell his congregation how he needs the money to fight the homosexuals. It always works. Sex turns people on. It opens their wallets, too."

The Reverend Renalski waited to see if anyone else wanted to respond.

"Are we agreed then," Reverend Renalski asked, "to do something about this problem in our city?'"

Heads bobbed in agreement.

"I'm with you," one man said, "but I want a guarantee that I won't get caught myself."

"You don't have to get 'caught,'" Renalski said. "There are people in this city who – how shall we say – who do things for – what shall we say – a certain consideration."

There was a grunt of disapproval.

"There's no reason why we cannot offer a few dollars to others to do what is necessary. And Halloween is a good time. They'll all be in one place and it will be so much easier. Can you imagine the sight: hundreds of jackrabbits scattering in every direction from a large hall? A simple bomb scare would do it."

Everyone laughed.

"Oh, I get it!" the man at the window said. "Halloween. Everybody will have masks on. Some of our people can get inside that hall. Nobody will know they don't belong. I get it now."

"But I think we should be clear about it: there's a difference between violence and merely scaring somebody. All we're doing is using Halloween to scare some people," Renalski insisted. "And after all, isn't that the traditional purpose of Halloween? Ghosts and goblins? Scaring people? Aren't we interested in restoring traditional values? What finer way to help that group prepare for All Saints' Day on November first."

"I'm forced to agree with Gordan here," said the priest. "When I was a boy growing up, I never even heard the word gay or homosexual. Those who didn't marry and raise families were recognized as queer. But now look at the world. Queers are actually coming out and demanding rights. Traditional values are crumbling. If we allow it to go on, there's no telling where it will stop. I'm afraid if gays are ever given rights, it will signal the total collapse of our civilization. That's why we have an obligation to stop them. It's our Christian duty to force them off the streets."

"Indeed it is," the Reverend Renalski returned gravely.

"But isn't your own son living with them?"

"Yes. That's why I'm anxious to take care of this."

"Will he be at the Halloween Party?"

"Yes. He assured me he's going. It's important that he realize how dangerous it is to continue associating with those people. He won't listen to me anymore. My only wish is to have him return to a normal lifestyle."

"What if somebody gets hurt?"

"There you go again. No one will be hurt," Renalski repeated. "How many times do I have to tell you that? Our only goal is to throw a scare into those queers to put them in their place once and for all. All agreed?"

No objections were raised.

"Well, it certainly has my blessing," intoned the preacher. "Now that's settled, perhaps we should turn it over to Loren."

"My first thought," Pritchind began, "is to plant some of our own people inside the building. We should have a field day at that pansy ball of theirs. But another possibility that comes to mind is the school behind the hall where they'll be holding the thing. If they could be accused of vandalism, can you see the headlines: GAYS DEMOLISH SCHOOL BUILDING."

"Remember," interrupted one of the clerics. "No violence. And to my mind, that also means no vandalsim or destruction of property."

"That's right. That's right. You're perfectly correct," Pritchind admitted. "Forget that about school vandalism. You're right; there should be no vandalism."

"There's an ancient adage I think we should recall," interjected Renalski. "Never let your right hand know what your left hand is planning. I think that should apply to Loren's plans for Halloween. Maybe it's best if we don't know exactly what Loren plans. We can't be blamed for what we don't know, can we? Let Loren contact the people who will do the actual, physical work. That way our hands will be clean. Is that all right with you, Loren?"

"My pleasure," replied Pritchind, grinning. "And I'll see to it that our – let's call them helpers – do not know who hired them."

"Gentlemen," Renalski said in summation, "our meeting this afternoon has been most productive. Before we adjourn, I suggest we rise and bow our heads in prayer. The Lord has blessed this gathering."

"Praise the Lord," exclaimed one man.

After a moment of silent thanksgiving, the Reverend Renalski led the group in the Lord's Prayer.

19

An unseasonably hot sun beat down upon the city on the thirty-first of October. Shortly after midday a light wind sprang up, spreading no cooling breeze across town but only its sultry humidity. Unusual weather, everybody said; no one could remember an autumn of such oppressive heat. And here it was Halloween.

When Matt can home from work and parked his old Chevy in front of the duplex, several other men were on the street, barechested and barefooted, washing their cars as if it were midsummer. Matt waved to them, and they returned the silent greeting, as he walked away from his car.

"Hey! Hey! Remember me?" Matt stopped, turning round.

A blond-haired young man ran up to him, his familiar face beaming.

"Remember me? From the hospital? I'm Harley. Your lover and me shared the same hospital room."

Matt remembered.

"What brings you to the neighborhood?" he asked.

"I was over at The Center the other night and met some guy who teaches in one of them goddam night schools. We started jawing and I find out he's got a real good job and he teaches in them goddam night schools for fun. Then – and you're not gonna believe this – he starts bawlin' me out just like I was his kid. He told me I should be ashamed for not doin' somethin' with my life. No lie, he yelled at me just like I was his son. Man, that never happened to be before. I mean, t'have somebody really take an interest in my future. God damn, that made me feel good! So he tells me to stop around sometime and he'd give me a bunch of papers to sign up and get started in some of their goddam classes, so here I am. Says I may need some goddam English classes. He lives down in that end house."

Harley, grinning broadly, pointed to the end of the street.

"When do your classes start?" Matt asked.

"Hell, I dunno. Wouldn't that be somethin' if I ever got enrolled in one of them goddam night schools!"

Harley's eyes danced at the prospect.

"What does your mom think about it?" Matt asked.

"I was gonna tell her last night when I got home but she had some guy with her and I didn't want to break it up . . . if ya know what I mean. But she'll be happy. I know that."

"Stop by sometime and let us know how you're doing. Jim and I live right here." Matt pointed up at the blue house with its crayfish on the porch.

"I may just do that. If I'm leisurin' around sometime I just may come over and let ya know how things are goin' for me," Harley said. "But once I start school and everythin' I may not have too much goddam time for myself."

Harley went on his way. Matt had stepped onto the sidewalk when a dark blue van with three workmen inside drew to a stop at the curb. The driver called out to him.

"Can you tell us where 704 is?"

"Second house from the corner," Matt directed.

"We can't see any numbers on these houses."

"I guess some of them are covered up by the murals," Matt apologized.

"We're house painters," one of the three explained, "and tomorrow we begin work on the inside of 704. That's the empty one, isn't it?"

"I don't know."

"Yeah, that's it," said another. "We're bringing our ladders, drop cloths, and paint over to the house this afternoon. That way we can start bright and early tomorrow morning."

There was a whispered conference inside the van.

"Hey buddy," the driver called again to Matt. "Seeing how we're in the neighborhood, do you want your apartment painted?"

"No need. The paint's holding up well."

"We do a good job. Not very expensive. And it's guaranteed. We could do it this week yet."

"I don't think so. If the owner wants it painted, he can do it."

"Suit yourself."

Matt nodded as the van eased up in front of 704. The men began unloading their painting equipment.

Matt sprinted up the wooden stairway two steps at a time. Even though Jim had opened all the windows, the air inside the apartment was stuffy, and had a stale smell. Jim, stretched out on the sofa before the television, wore only a pair of cut-off jeans. His shoulders were lightly sunburned.

"Who was that you were talking to? In the van, I mean."

"Some painters. They'll be working a couple doors down the street. Start tomorrow."

"Suppose Marie ever got the bedrooms painted?" Jim asked.

"No. She hates to paint."

"Funny, isn't it?"

"What?"

"That morning, all that mattered was measuring the walls; then, that afternoon, those walls were the last thing that mattered."

Matt stood staring into space for a moment. "I ran into Harley. He's going back to school."

"I'm glad. Hope it works out. It's time he gets a break."

"Been outside?" Matt called over his shoulder on his way into the bedroom. "You look a little red."

"Spent the afternoon outside," Jim shouted back. "Thought it would do me some good before going back to work next week."

"Pick up our costumes for the Masquerade Party tonight?" Matt asked.

"Don't know if I'm going," Jim said.

Matt appeared in the bedroom doorway.

"What do you mean, you don't know if you're going? I thought it was all settled."

"That's why I went outside this afternoon. To get the costume. Then I walked down the street and talked to the guys out washing their cars. Wore me out. Guess I'm not up to any physical exertion yet. You understand, don't you?"

"I was counting on your being up and around by tonight. I thought we'd go, you know, together."

"But I want you to go. I'm just not up to it."

"I sure wasn't expecting to go alone," Matt complained.

"As soon as you get there you'll be with people you know."

"Maybe I should stay here with you."

"That would make me feel worse. Put on your costume. Go on. I don't want you to miss it. It'll be quite an experience for you." Jim insisted. "I know – why not ask Willie? Maybe you two can go together," Jim encouraged.

Matt glanced from Jim to the telephone then back to Jim.

"Go on. Give him a call," Jim urged.

Matt went to the phone and dialed the number Jim dictated.

"Willie? Jim doesn't feel up to going to the Halloween Party tonight. Want to go with me?... Oh, I see.... When did you meet him?... No, never mind. That's all right. Maybe I'll see you tonight."

Matt hung up the receiver.

"Well?" Jim asked.

"Willie said somebody else asked him to go."

"Who?"

"Somebody he met last week at the Shattersheen Party. Remember?" Matt said testily. "You didn't feel like going to that party either."

Jim didn't answer.

Matt had to admit that, despite the sunburn he had got earlier in the afternoon, Jim still looked pale. But his experience had wrought greater changes in Jim than his sickly pallor: his ordinarily outgoing nature had grown subdued, leaving him tense and anxious about leaving the house, as if distrustful of all strangers.

Neither Matt nor Jim had much to say as they ate supper. The wind had shifted direction, slamming doors shut from sudden gusts and whipping the curtains at every window.

Matt got up, walked to the front window of the apartment and looked at the sky: no rain clouds. Only the wind blowing. He pulled the window down and immediately the curtains limply fell to their original position. He made a quick circuit through the apartment closing the windows and when he returned to the kitchen table the air within the apartment had grown still and the stale odor of musty upholstery filled his nostrils once again.

"By the way," Jim said, "I called the admissions office over at the college today. I have an appointment tomorrow afternoon at two o'clock."

"That's good," Matt smiled. "Glad to hear it."

"We talked on the phone for a couple minutes. They suggested I start off easy in January when the new semester begins. Since I'll only be going part-time maybe one course will be enough for the first semester. That way, I'll learn the ropes and get used to studying again."

Pausing, Jim asked, "Want to take a course with me?"

"Maybe, maybe. I never thought about going to college, but I guess it couldn't hurt to try one course."

"Maybe by January things will start to work out for both of us," Jim offered.

"How's that?"

"Oh, I mean if I could get started in college. And if everything gets resolved with your divorce."

Immediately after supper Matt began to dress for the party. His costume for the masquerade was that of a pirate. Not since his kindergarten days had he donned such an outfit as his pirate's costume. A bright red kerchief tied round his neck hung down the strip of chest left bare by his white, open-fronted silk shirt. Snug dark breeches were tucked into knee-high boots, and in a leather sheath on his wide black belt hung a long knife.

His mask in hand, Matt stood at the bedroom door and called to Jim who lay again on the sofa watching television.

"How do I look?"

Jim jumped up.

"You shouldn't take this," he cautioned, clutching the knife sheathed at Matt's side. "If a cop stops you, he'll bust you for carrying a weapon. Especially tonight."

Matt glanced down at the knife then looked intently at Jim.

"I'm serious," Jim insisted. "I'd leave it here if I were you."

Matt unsnapped the button holding the sheath to his belt and returned the knife to a drawer in the bedroom.

"Now, put on your mask," Jim suggested.

"Aw," Matt grumbled.

"Go on. I want to see how it looks."

Slipping the thin rubber mask over his head, Matt was transformed into the archetypal pirate. With its protruding eyeballs, cruel mouth, bloody gashes, fearsome scars – the false face was graphic in every detail.

"Looks good," Jim said approvingly. "Authentic."

The mask fit Matt's face so well that it reflected his every facial movement. He stood still as Jim inspected it from all angles, then pulled it off his head.

"Sorry I'm not going with you," said Jim wistfully.

Jim gazed at Matt's wide-open shirt-front then raised his hand to rub it gently across Matt's chest. Jim's fingers and palm slowly slid back and forth across the muscled chest.

Matt stood motionless.

"Feels good," he moaned softly.

"I wish *I* felt better," Jim said. "I'd really like to go but I know I wouldn't have a good time. I don't have the energy yet."

"Next year," Matt encouraged. "We can go together next year."

With his right hand, Matt drew his fingers across Jim's forehead and swept the hair back.

"Your lip's all healed," Matt said brushing with his finger the place where the cut had been. "There isn't even a scar."

Jim's arms encircled Matt's back and their faces drew close together as they embraced in silence for many moments.

Matt drew away and moved to the door. He turned on the threshold. "I'll probably be home sometime after midnight."

He closed the door and was gone.

Jim walked into the bathroom and let the cold water run a few seconds before he filled the plastic cup. He reached for the bottle of tablets prescribed for pain when he left the hospital, opened the small vial and shook one of the tablets onto his palm. After swallowing the pill, he went to the couch and settled himself for an evening of quiet rest, watching television. Within minutes the medication took effect, making him drowsy. Soon his mind and body would relax into a deep sleep.

Stepping outside Matt was struck by a blast of wind which blew into his open shirt-front, filling out the soft silk material like a balloon. Fallen leaves hurtled through the air like miniature projectiles as he hurried down the steps to his car. Most of the houses on the street were already dark because the men had gone off to their Halloween parties, the Masquerade Party the destination of most. A single sheet of newspaper had blown flat against the windshield of his Chevy and Matt paused to peel it off before getting into the car. The house at the end of the street was brightly lit; the painters working late apparently, setting up their equipment for the morning.

Matt drove to the party hall and was directed into the parking lot by two city policemen. He felt a bit foolish walking past them after getting out of his car to enter the hall. Not since childhood had he dressed in any kind of costume. And here he was on the street wearing a pirate's outfit.

Stepping into the hall Matt found it already filled with pilgrims and princesses, monsters and monks, cops and clowns, bodybuilders in the briefest of straps and drag queens in the most lavish of silks. Satins and brocades rubbed against leather and denim as unsmiling men wearing open-front chaqueta jackets mingled with rouged and giggling queens. Matt watched the costumed revelers and listened to the din of music and shouting. This was his first masquerade party. The placid "trick or treat" of his Willow Glen childhood could not compare with the sights and sounds unfolding before him.

Inside the front door new arrivals to the party were given ticket stubs for door prizes and number cards for the costumes.

"Buy your ticket here, honey," called out a husky voice emanating from a man dressed in a nun's habit. The nun was assisted in the sale of tickets by a man wearing only an eye mask, a red T-shirt, sky blue briefs, and white sneakers. Lettered on his shirt-front were the words "BROTHER EVERHARD"; the back read "REPENT – THE END IS HERE," below which an arrow pointed downward.

Matt pulled out his wallet and fumbled for a bill.

"Large crowd, huh?" Matt said.

"Oh honey, we expect a packed house before the night's over," the nun replied.

"Will you be competing in the striptease contest later on?" asked Brother Everhard.

"Uh... no... I don't think so," Matt answered.

"Wouldn't you know it," the man said. "The ones you hope will keep on every stitch are always the first ones who want to strip. And the ones you'd like to see *au naturel* have a Victorian complex every time."

"I like your costume," Matt offered to the nun.

"Oh you *are* a dear. It's appropriate, though. Without priests and nuns I would never have learned what a masquerade religion can be."

"Huh?"

"Oh honey, you're a real sweetie!"

Newcomers surging into the building behind Matt swept him into the hall.

The crowded dance floor was lined with tables where men sat eating and drinking amid the din. To the rear a live band was performing on stage; their name, painted on the large bass drum, was The Crowin' Cocks. Matt's eyes were drawn to the far corner of the stage where a young man had jumped up and begun an impromptu striptease. A small group had gathered round below the stage, clapping in unison and cheering him on. Turning now his back, now his face to the crowd he gyrated to the music, unfastening his fly between bumps and grinds. As the group below him shouted their approval, the young man quickly pushed his pants down and pulled them up again. The group cheered again, more faintly than before, then drifted away from the stage as if disappointed by the spectacle although the music continued unabated.

Suddenly someone grabbed Matt by the hand and pulled him onto the dance floor. His abductor wore a black mask, a skintight yellow T-shirt and the skimpiest bikini briefs. Tossed together on the crowded floor, Matt and his partner danced closer and closer until finally their arms enfolded, the man's hands gliding over Matt's chest. Caught up in the frenzy of the dancing, Matt let his hand fall to his partner's briefs. Then the music stopped as the rafters reverberated with the applause and cheering that rose up from the throng. His abductor disappeared in the crowd and Matt did not see him again.

Matt pulled the hot rubber mask from his head and passed his hand over his brow to remove the sweat that had beaded there. He felt a hand on his shoulder.

"Glad you could make it. Where's Jim?"

Matt turned and though a narrow mask covered the eyes, Matt recognized Richard's voice.

"He decided at the last minute not to come," Matt shouted above the music, which had begun again. "Said he wasn't up to it. When we were back at the apartment I didn't understand why, but I sure do now."

Richard smiled. "I know it's a party, but could I see you privately for a minute – where it's less noisy?"

Matt motioned to the nearby stage door.

Outside the hall the howling wind diminished the noise and music within to a dull throb.

"When you get home," Richard explained, "you can tell Jim that all those zoning questions about The Center have been resolved. The people causing the problems suddenly stopped their opposition. I got a call from the mayor's office telling me that the matter had been taken care of and we had nothing to worry about."

While Richard talked, the distant wail of sirens was borne faintly upon the night air. Far away at first, they grew more distinct until both Richard and Matt turned to look down the street.

"You don't think the police are raiding us, do you?" Matt asked.

Richard shook his head. "I thought we had everything cleared."

A police cruiser with lights flashing and siren blaring sped nearer the hall followed by two fire trucks. Air horns blasted sharp, ear-splitting warnings as the fire trucks raced down the street toward the school behind the party hall.

"At least it's not a raid," Matt laughed, as the emergency equipment continued past them.

"As I was saying," Richard repeated, "give Jim that message. We talked about it the other day when I was at your place."

More flashing lights split the darkness of the street. This time two police cruisers were followed by an ambulance. Sirens echoed elsewhere in the city.

"Look!" Matt said. "Maybe we spoke too fast."

A police cruiser pulled up to the parking lot beside the party hall, blocking the driveway entrance, its lights flashing. An officer leaned out to speak briefly with the two city policemen directing traffic into the lot. Matt and Richard walked toward them.

"Traffic has to be rerouted around the area," yelled the officer to the patrolmen.

"What's the matter?" Richard called out to the traffic cops.

"Fire."

"Where?"

"Gay ghetto."

20

The police drove off.

"Let's take my car," Richard said. "It's parked right here."

In seconds Richard and Matt were out of the lot and onto the street heading toward the gay ghetto.

On the way, Richard had to pull the car to the curb several times and wait for emergency vehicles to pass. As they approached the gay ghetto, the sky flared neon-red.

"Which street do you suppose it's on?" Matt asked nervously.

Richard didn't answer.

When they came closer to the gay district they saw not only glow in the sky, but also smoke curling over the rooftops in the neighborhood.

Many blocks from Matt's duplex a city police officer was rerouting traffic. The cop was holding a red flare, directing traffic, and pointing in the opposite direction of the fire. Short, shrill blasts from the whistle dangling in his mouth reinforced his hand signals. He did not allow Richard to enter the area.

Richard turned his car onto a side street. He and Matt jumped out, racing toward Matt's street. Exercise and anxiety caused Matt to break out in a sweat. He tugged at the red kerchief around his neck, throwing it and his mask into the gutter as he ran along the sidewalk. They were still three blocks from his duplex. Flames occasionally licked the darkness, but he could not yet see which house was on fire.

At the last corner, a cluster of people blocked their path. A crowd of onlookers had already gathered behind the police cordon.

Matt forgot Richard. He pushed his way to the street. Jostled from right to left, he elbowed his way through the throng.

Reaching a point which gave him a clear view down the street, Matt stared at the fire. Three houses at the end of the street were engulfed in flames and the side wall of the fourth house was already burning.

Flames swirled into the sky, their embers like burning matches raining down on neighboring houses. Fire hoses sprayed jets of water on rooftops where embers were burning.

Matt cupped his right hand above his eyes to see better.

The fire swelled. The wind blew in different directions. One moment the street was shrouded in billows of smoke pouring from the buildings; the next moment, the street was brilliantly illuminated as flaming crimson flashes ate through the smoke. The only constant lights were those flashing atop the fire trucks and the searchlight beams scanning housefronts for occupants trapped within.

Any noise from the spectators was drowned out by the constant hissing of water striking the flame. Crackling explosions erupted from timbers as fire devoured whole rooms. Only the bullhorn-transmitted orders of the fire chief could be heard above the din.

Matt tugged at a cop's sleeve. "Is everybody out? Did you get everybody out?"

"The first alarm was for a fire at a vacant house down there at 704. But by the time I got here, two other houses were already burning. There may have been some people in one of them."

"Did they get everybody out?"

"There was an evacuation, door to door. They got a couple people out. Some in the crowd now, watching. Some were removed to hospitals."

"How'd it start?"

"The fire marshal decides that, buddy."

"Any idea?" Matt shouted back.

"Whenever a fire gets started that good it's usually an explosion. But that's a guess. Don't quote me."

"Did they get Jim out?" Matt yelled. "Is Jim safe?"

"Sorry buddy," the police officer said. "I don't even know who Jim is."

The intensity of the heat was forcing firefighters to move their trucks onto side streets. Even the crowd was voluntarily moving back. First a few steps. Then many more feet away from the heat. Smoke rolled off the fire in choking waves. First, high into the air then low along the ground, directly toward the onlookers.

"All unauthorized personnel evacuate the area immediately," the voice grated. "Police are asked to remove all unauthorized personnel from the area."

Matt called out to the officer again: "Where did the ambulance take the people. Which hospital are they at?"

"I dunno, pal. I only got one job. Crowd control."

Matt turned away, bumping into Richard.

"Let's find Jim," Matt said, scanning the crowd. "I don't see him here. I've got to find him."

"If he's standing somewhere watching the fire, there's no way of finding him," Richard said. "There are people all around."

As they fought their way back through the crowd, Matt and Richard heard an unusual noise. Matt paused.

The noise lasted not more than three seconds.

When Matt lived on the farm he heard this sound whenever he lit a gasoline-soaked brush pile in an open field. He'd strike a match, throw it on the pile, and the sudden draft of wind rushing into the pile with the igniting gasoline would cause a brief, rumbling clap, like a miniature explosion.

The sound he heard now was the same, but magnified hundreds of times. The street vibrated and a popping sound hurt his eardrums. Women screamed. Without turning to look, Matt knew what had happened.

The dry timber of the closely-built houses, the extended drought, the intensity of the wind: a firestorm was ripping through the block-long row of houses with the fury of an explosion.

The street erupted into a tunnel of flames.

Though the spectators stood far from the fire, the sudden burst of flames made them run in the opposite direction.

Before getting into the car, Matt glanced back for only a second to where his blue house with its crayfish mural had stood. Walls of flame were whipping skyward as if to scorch the clouds on this Halloween night.

Richard drove to the closest pay telephone. He called police headquarters and asked the name of the hospital to which the fire victims had been taken. Richard jumped back in the car and they headed for City Hospital.

Milling around the entrance to the hospital emergency room were costumed men from the Masquerade Party. They came directly to the hospital when they heard of the fire. Standing in small clusters, they anxiously spoke with each other on the sidewalk. Richard and Matt hurried past them into the hospital.

A security guard at the entrance recognized Richard. "Several victims are back there," the guard said as he pointed to the trauma rooms behind the double doors. "We don't have ID's on them. If you could help with identification, we'd appreciate it."

Richard hurried in.

The security guard walked with Richard past the gathered visitors and bystanders. Hospital personnel were fast at work among the cubicles. Matt followed at a short distance.

For the first time since leaving the Masquerade Party Matt looked down at himself and his bizarre clothing. Brow moist with sweat, the odor of smoke clung to his body and costume.

Both Richard and Matt recognized two men lying in different cubicles. They lived in the corner house on Matt's street. As neither was conscious Richard gave their names and addresses to the guard.

The guard led Richard to another cubicle. It was separated from the others by a long white curtain drawn between the beds. Matt looked at the figure lying there surrounded by mechanical lifesaving equipment.

"Hi."

Harley's monosyllable was barely audible.

The sharp, pungent odor of burned flesh hovered in the air. Doctors attending Harley blocked out Matt's view.

A nurse turned to Matt. "Sir, you'll have to leave this area. Only hospital personnel are allowed here."

Matt turned quickly and walked out of the room.

"Of the five people in there I knew four. I couldn't recognize the fifth," Richard commented as he joined Matt in the corridor.

"Let's get out of here," Matt said. "Let's get back to the crowds of sightseers at the fire. I've got to find Jim. He isn't here at the hospital."

"Stay here for a few moments while I walk over to the other side of the building," Richard suggested.

Richard talked with two security guards. After Richard left with one, Matt asked the other, "What's on the other side of the hospital? Another emergency room?"

"Morgue. That's where the hospital morgue is."

Matt looked inside the cubicles again and saw that the doctors and nurses surrounding Harley had stopped their work.

One doctor paused momentarily.

"We just lost him. Have someone contact the next of kin for Harley

Robbins." The doctor glanced at the wall clock. "Time of death was 1:17 a.m."

Matt walked down the corridor to the visitors' waiting room and he slumped into a chair. He leaned forward and buried his head in his hands.

Time slowed to a standstill. Matt thought the clock on the wall had stopped but as he glanced up at it again, he could see the second hand revolving in its slow, silent orbit. It was twenty-five minutes past one.

When two people brushed his chair and stopped in front of it, Matt's eyes swept past the clock and focused on the figures who stood before him. He looked into the face of Dr. Denison. Richard stood at his side.

"I'm sorry Matt. You have my deepest sympathy."

But for a volley of eye contact tentatively made and flinchingly withdrawn, the three men's faces remained expressionless.

"The paramedics administered emergency treatment all the way to the hospital, but he had already taken in too much smoke," Dr. Denison was saying. "There isn't a burn mark on his body. It was smoke inhalation. Apparently he collapsed while trying to get out. He was found inside the door to your apartment."

Matt's eyes studied the doctor's dangling stethoscope for a long time, then he rose from his chair as if to leave but remained still as if paralyzed.

"How many victims altogether?" Richard asked quietly.

"Two confirmed dead. Four injured; two critically. I called the police chief just a minute ago to verify that all residents had been evacuated and he assured me they were, that all the residents are accounted for from those houses. We're getting some firefighters now. Some of their injuries may be life-threatening. I don't know yet.'"

"Does anybody know how it started?" Richard asked.

"It's sketchy yet," Dr. Denison admitted, "but I talked to the police to get some idea of the kinds of injuries we'd be getting. They said a call came into police headquarters around ten o'clock that a house in the 700 block had literally blown apart. Some kind of explosion. The fire marshal will rule on the exact cause. As soon as the first house blew, the houses on either side caught fire."

"I knew that Harley Robbins wasn't going to the Masquerade Party till later in the evening," Richard said irrelevantly. "He told me about a week ago that he didn't have the money to rent a costume, but that he wanted to stop by later in the evening for the party and dancing.

"And why was Harley Robbins anywhere near that house when it blew apart? Harley lives way over on Fifteenth Street."

His consciousness stirred, Matt tried to open his mouth to explain, but no words came to his lips. Denison answered.

"One of the men who lives in that corner house told me just before we took him into surgery that Harley Robbins was at their house tonight filling out some papers. I really didn't know what he was talking about."

"Will the two men pull through?" Richard asked.

Dr. Denison held up crossed fingers on both hands.

"Do you want to stay here, Matt? Or go back to The Center with me?" Richard asked.

Matt mouthed the word no.

"There will be a place for you down at The Center for as long as you need, Matt," Richard said. "Is there anything I can do? Anything?"

Matt looked around the waiting room as though searching for some unknown, unrecognized object. He appeared oblivious to Dr. Denison's presence or to Richard's offer.

He walked away from Richard and Dr. Denison down the corridor.

As Matt left the building, an ambulance had just arrived at the emergency entrance. He silently stood to the side as he watched a firefighter wheeled into the hospital on a stretcher. The firefighter was not moving.

Matt looked in the direction of his old neighborhood. The former red brilliance of the sky above had been replaced by giant clouds of white-gray smoke. The wind was not as strong as it had been earlier in the evening but in its sporadic gusts the crackling of the fire was borne toward the hospital. Directions to firefighters and police officers were faintly audible. Wailing sirens from firefighting equipment floated through the night air. The knoll on which the hospital stood seemed so distant from the fire, so far removed from the destruction and death its staff now tried to mend.

Matt walked down the front sidewalk from the hospital and watched the city lights flickering like candles over the intact sectors of the city. He thought of his '68 Chevy still parked in the lot beside the hall where the Masquerade Party had been held and wondered if anyone remained at the hall. Many costumed men had been at the scene of the fire, watching it in silence. Now others, scattered in groups and still talking quietly, approached the entrance to the hospital. They were joined by a flock of curiosity seekers.

"Have they released the names yet of those who were injured?"

asked a costumed man who had just arrived on the scene. He wasn't speaking to anyone in particular; the question was addressed to anyone who would answer.

"I heard that every one of the bodies is so badly burned it will be days before they know any names," someone said with assurance.

"I heard somebody say they brought more than a dozen critically injured here, all from the same house," a conservatively dressed woman said. "And you know what else? I heard every victim was under fourteen years old and each was chained to a bed. I guess those poor kids were bought and sold like slaves."

"Those queers are really sick," said her male companion as they walked past the costumed men. "It's just as well all that trash burned. It's just a damned shame all those innocent kids were hurt, too."

Matt left the sidewalk and broke into a run, across the lawn in front of the hospital, to the far end of the street. There, away from the rumors and invective, he could grieve.

21

November brought the rains that October had never produced. The steady rains that began the day after Halloween continued intermittently throughout the first two weeks of the month. Even on those days when it did not rain, the sky remained overcast and heavy with dark gray clouds threatening to burst anew and drench the earth with more water. There was a winter sharpness to the November damp. Neither the black trunks of the leafless trees nor the wet fields, now harvested and bare, relieved the oppressive gray of the landscape. Indian summer had vanished without a trace.

On Sunday, the tenth of November, the small white church in Willow Glen was shrouded in mist. On the sodden lawn, a neat handlettered sign had been tacked inside the glass-fronted announcement board:

Memorial Service
for
James Renalski
November 10   11:00 a.m.

A chill drizzle had been falling as the bells tolled at eleven o'clock but sometime during the service the rain stopped. When the church choir began the recessional hymn patches of the sidewalk and parking area had begun to dry, and breaks in the clouds gave hope the sun might show itself before day's end.

When the church doors opened, many members of the congregation began filing past the preacher. But many familiar faces Matt had expected to see at the Sunday morning service were nowhere to be seen. Marie was not there. Neither were her father and brothers. There were other members of the congregation who chose not to come to church this morning, but in their place had come many strangers. Jim's friends from the city had driven the distance to attend the service and their presence warmed the small church this damp morning.

Matt was delayed in leaving the building. Mr. Caffrey was immediately in front of him and the old man's steps required the use of a cane. The elderly gentleman inched his way down the aisle, holding on to each pew with his free hand. It was not until he reached the door that he turned and saw Matt.

"You probably know, Matt, I lost three sons. Two in Korea. Then my third boy ran off to Canada. So I know how it feels to lose somebody. Matt, I don't have any idea what it's like to be gay – I never even heard the word till people around here started talking – but if losing that young man was as much a loss to you as my three boys were to me, well...."

By way of conclusion, Mr. Caffrey patted Matt on the shoulder then turned and slowly made his way down the church steps.

Tom, a former high school classmate of Matt's, bypassed the preacher and stepped alongside Matt.

"Why did you even return to Willow Glen?" Tom asked. "This town is better off without people like you. And why did you bring all that trash from the city? I don't like to go to church only to be reminded that there are people like you in the world."

"Maybe it's time congregations were reminded that there are people in the world like me," Matt said.

Tom hurried past.

"Do you live in Willow Glen?" The preacher spoke to Matt.

"I lived here all my life. It was only this past summer I moved away."

"Did you know the young man for whom the memorial service was held?"

"Yes. We were good friends. Lovers, really. I'm Matt Justin."

"Oh, I see," the preacher said thoughtfully. "Tragic death. Tragic. For everyone involved. I'm only here temporarily from the seminary. Until the people can find a full-time pastor. I wish my words could erase the hurt you most certainly feel. If there's anything I can do to help...."

"He wasn't even nineteen," Matt said abstractedly.

"I beg your pardon," the preacher said.

"Tomorrow Jim would have been nineteen."

The minister did not offer any words at first, but Matt's wide, hurt eyes seemed to demand an answer.

"His death may have accomplished what his life could not," the minister said.

Matt's gaze remained fastened on the minister's eyes.

"Unless there's a reason for dying, there's little point in living, is there?"

"Jim didn't choose to die," Matt answered.

"Are you sure?"

"He was killed."

"Every life has risks. Without risks, nothing is ever achieved. Jim accepted those risks. He led his life as fully as possible."

"Why should it be a risk to be honest about yourself?" Matt asked, his eyes scanning the surrounding hillsides.

"Hasn't his death made you confront the realities of your own life?"

"Is that the only reason for living?" Matt asked. "To help others confront life?"

"When violence robs life from those we love, a part of us dies with them. But another part of us is waiting to be born. Hope for the living is often born in the courage of the dying. Religion is that inner hope, that inner courage."

"Religion destroyed Jim," Matt said.

"Was it religion?" the minister asked, "or someone who misused religion?"

The minister extended his hand to Matt. His grasp was strong, genuine.

Matt smiled feebly.

He moved away, leaving the preacher to greet other members of the congregation.

As if from nowhere a teenage girl suddenly stood beside Matt. She tugged at his arm.

"Do you remember me? Do you?" she asked.

Matt's puzzled expression changed to recognition.

"Ellen. Your name's Ellen. The Fourth of July picnic."

She thrust a small hymnal into Matt's hands.

"What's this?" Matt asked.

"We sat beside each other in choir. This is my very own hymnal and I always shared it with him. I want you to have it. My parents said I shouldn't come to the memorial service this morning, but I got ready and came anyway. I told Momma that whatever she said or thought, he was nice to me. He really was."

She vanished as quickly as she had appeared, and Matt was left holding the hymnal Jim had used at church services.

He remained standing on the church steps as he tucked the small book into his overcoat pocket. His eyes glanced across the crowd till they settled on Letty, the wife of the Reverend Gordan Renalski. She was standing alone on the church lawn.

When they came face to face no words were exchanged but they hugged each other for many moments, causing several members of the congregation to avert their eyes as they walked briskly past.

She loosened her grasp on Matt. Placing his hand on her shoulders, he looked at her intently.

"What now?" he asked. "How do we go on?"

"I'm not sure. Even if I wanted to stay in Willow Glen I can't make a living here. So I'll probably move on. Gordan's resigned from the ministry. He is devastated. So am I."

"What about your personal life?" Matt asked. "What about your marriage?"

"May God forgive me," said Letty, "but I hope it's over. I spoke with Gordan on the phone several days ago. We talked about a separation. Divorce, perhaps. There's no way we can live together any longer."

"I'm sorry for you," Matt murmured.

"Have the police been in touch with you?" Letty asked.

"Yes. Many times. When I went to them and told them about the dark blue van, they felt sure it was the key to the fire. I volunteered to go under hypnosis to remember the license numbers. But I'm sure I never noticed them in the first place. I can't recall what I never saw. I gave the police descriptions of the men inside. They haven't been located so far."

"Do you think the culprits will ever be caught?" Letty asked.

Matt shook his head. "I don't know. I really don't."

"At least that Loren Pritchind lost the election," Letty said.

"That's some consolation," Matt answered.

"And Jim... I don't know that I'll ever get over the loss...." Letty did not continue. She turned her glance from Matt and stared vacantly into the hillsides surrounding Willow Glen.

"I'll keep in touch," Matt promised.

They embraced again.

Matt walked over to Richard and Dr. Denison. They were waiting near their car in the parking lot.

As Matt approached them, he caught sight of another car door opening. Marie got out and as she came toward Matt, the passenger door of her car opened and Greg jumped out and came running to Matt.

"Daddy! Daddy!" the child yelled. Matt stooped down and held out his arms.

Greg flung himself into his father's arms. Matt swooped him up and held him tightly.

"You've grown into quite a man since I left you last summer," Matt said.

"I'm not a man," Greg giggled. "I'm only a boy. A little boy."

Matt looked at his son and brushed the hair from his eyes.

"You coming home now?" Greg asked. "You've been gone a long, long time, Daddy."

"Have you missed me?" Matt asked.

Greg nodded.

"I've missed you, too." Matt held his son tighter and pressed his lips against the boy's forehead.

"Did your mother tell you yet about Christmas?"

The boy shook his head vigorously.

"What would you say if I told you the lawyer said...."

"What's a lawyer?" the boy interrupted.

"It's a person who's trying to help me and your mother work out a schedule so we can both see you."

The boy's eyes grew large.

"The lawyer told me that you can spend Christmas Eve and Christmas Day with your mother. But then, guess what?"

"What?" Greg repeated.

"I'll spend a couple days with you right after Christmas. Two days. Maybe even three. What do you think of that?"

"Yippee," the child screamed. "Wait till I tell Joey. He keeps telling me I don't have a daddy anymore."

Marie stood at a discreet distance while Matt and Greg spoke with each other, then she walked over to them.

"Greg's grown a lot," Matt said. "I'm glad you brought him."

"At first I didn't want to do this," Marie said. "I couldn't force myself to attend the service this morning. But Greg's been asking for you so much lately. I suspected you'd be here."

Husband and wife looked at each other, then looked away.

"Where will all those people live?" Marie asked.

"They've already started to rebuild. I want to help them rebuild."

"Why would you ever want to return and live with those people?"

"Because that's where I feel at home."

A look of puzzled incomprehension crossed Marie's face.

"For a couple days that's all they talked about on the news. The fire and all," Marie said. "I never told Greg it was where you lived. Didn't want to worry him."

"Thanks. I never even thought about him seeing it on television."

"Were you in that fire, Daddy?"

"No. I watched it. But I wasn't in it. I was safe on the street a couple blocks away."

"What's a block?" Greg asked, still in Matt's arms.

"About as far as the back porch to the edge of the meadow."

"Oh."

Matt stooped down until Greg's shoes touched the pavement. Bypassing the other children, Greg ran from Matt and Marie to play by himself in the front yard of the church.

"Don't you allow Greg to play with the other children in Sunday school?" Matt asked.

"Why do you say that?"

"He's all alone. Playing by himself. The other children are ignoring him."

"Children in large cities may learn tolerance," she answered crisply. "Children in small towns don't. They can be vicious and cruel. So can their parents."

Matt watched his son standing alone, apart from the other children.

"Doesn't he have any friends?" Matt asked.

"There's the McCutchin boy, Joey. Both kids are about the same age."

"Does McCutchin still come over and visit?"

"They wave. But they haven't neighbored since the day you left."

Matt lowered his eyes.

"Don't get the wrong idea," Marie said quickly. "Nothing's changed. Everything's the same. Between us, that is. But I thought maybe if Greg saw you, he'd quit complaining so much."

"You're wrong, Marie. Everything has changed."

She gave a toss of her head.

"After the property settlement," she began, "I may move away from here with Greg. I'd like a fresh start, too. Outside some big city, maybe."

As Marie turned away, she glanced at Matt's left hand. His wedding band was not on his finger.

Matt walked away toward the car in which Dr. Denison and Richard sat waiting for a word with him. He stopped before the open window.

"I appreciate your making the trip out to Willow Glen this morning," Matt said.

"Your wife?" Richard asked, looking toward Marie.

Matt nodded. "That's my son over there. Greg."

"Looks like his dad," Denison observed.

"While we're here is there anything we can do for you?" Richard asked.

"No, no thanks."

Matt watched as Richard and Dr. Denison slowly drove out of the parking lot and onto the road leading out of Willow Glen, then looked overhead. It was a winter sky, crisp and cold, but small patches of sunlight now raced between the clouds, illuminating the countryside.

Willie stood at his elbow. "Anybody else you want to talk with while you're here?"

Matt looked around the crowd.

"No. That about does it.... Ready to get started?" Matt asked.

Willie shrugged. "Whenever you are."

The two walked to the red foreign car parked in a corner of the lot.

Willie drove onto the road in front of the church and turned in the direction of Junction 235. Matt glanced back.

The wife of the former preacher walked back to the parsonage alone.

Marie stood waiting for Greg, arms crossed, her eyes following Willie's car.

Having lived away from Willow Glen for several months, Matt studied the village church as if with new eyes. It looked different: much smaller, smaller than he ever remembered it. As a child, Matt had looked upon the church as the largest building in Willow Glen. Now it appeared tiny, insignificant, useless.

Seeing his father wave from the car window, Greg ran to the edge of the parking lot. He raised his small hand and was still waving as the car rounded a bend in the country road.

Matt lowered his hand but continued looking out the window.

The church steeple loomed ever smaller as the church itself grew more distant. The very valley seemed to swallow the church edifice.

Finally, the church was lost from Matt's sight.

Also available from Alyson

Don't miss our *free* book offer at the end of this section.

☐ **ONE TEENAGER IN TEN: Writings by gay and lesbian youth,** edited by Ann Heron, $3.95. One teenager in ten is gay; here, twenty-six young people tell their stories: of coming to terms with being different, of the decision how – and whether – to tell friends and parents, and what the consequences were.

☐ **SWEET DREAMS,** by John Preston, $4.95. Who says heroes can't be gay? Not John Preston. In his new Alex Kane series, he has created a gay alternative to The Destroyer and The Executioner – a crusader against homophobia, whose only weakness is other men.

☐ **THE BUTTERSCOTCH PRINCE,** by Richard Hall, $4.95. When Cordell's best friend and ex-lover is murdered, the only clue is one that the police seem to consider too kinky to follow up on. So Cordell decides to track down the killer himself – with results far different from what he had expected.

☐ **A DIFFERENT LOVE,** by Clay Larkin, $4.95. There have been heterosexual romance novels for years; now here's a gay one. When Billy and Hal meet in a small midwestern town, they feel sure that their love for each other is meant to last. But then they move to San Francisco, and the temptations of city life create complications they haven't had to face before.

☐ **THE ALEXANDROS EXPEDITION,** by Patricia Sitkin, $5.95. When Evan Talbot leaves on a mission to rescue an old schoolmate who has been imprisoned by fanatics in the Middle East, he doesn't realize that the trip will also involve his own coming out and the discovery of who it is that he really loves.

☐ **DANNY,** by Margaret Sturgis, $6.95. High school teacher Tom York has a problem when the school board wants to censor many of the books he feels are most important for his classes to read. But all that pales in the face of the new difficulties that arise when he finds himself in an intense love affair with Danny, his most promising student.

☐ **$TUD,** by Phil Andros; introduction by John Preston, $6.95. Phil Andros is a hot and horny hustler with a conscience, pursuing every form of sex – including affection – without apology, yet with a sense of humor and a golden rule philosophy. When Sam Steward wrote these stories back in the sixties, they elevated gay fiction to new heights; today they remain as erotic and delightful as ever.

☐ **THE SPARTAN,** by Don Harrison, $5.95. In the days of the first Olympics, gay relationships were a common and valued part of life. *The Spartan* tells the story of a young athlete and his adventures in love and war, providing a vivid picture of classical Greece, the early Olympics, and an important part of our history.

☐ **REFLECTIONS OF A ROCK LOBSTER: A story about growing up gay,** by Aaron Fricke, $4.95. When Aaron Fricke took a male date to the senior prom, no one was surprised: he'd gone to court to be able to do so, and the case had made national news. Here Aaron tells his story, and shows what gay pride can mean in a small New England town.

☐ **COMING OUT RIGHT, A handbook for the gay male,** by Wes Muchmore and William Hanson, $5.95. The first steps into the gay world – whether it's a first relationship, a first trip to a gay bar, or coming out at work – can be full of unknowns. This book will make it easier. Here is advice on all aspects of gay life for both the inexperienced and the experienced.

Get this book free!

When were you last outraged by prejudiced media coverage of gay people? Chances are it hasn't been long. *Talk Back!* tells how you, in surprisingly little time, can do something about it.

If you order at least three other books from us, you may request a FREE copy of this important book. (See order form on next page.)

To get these books:

Ask at your favorite bookstore for the books listed here. You may also order by mail. Just fill out the coupon below, or use your own paper if you prefer not to cut up this book.

GET A FREE BOOK! When you order any three books listed here at the regular price, you may request a *free* copy of *Talk Back!*

BOOKSTORES: Standard trade terms apply. Details and catalog available on request.

Send orders to: **Alyson Publications, Inc.**
PO Box 2783, Dept. B-52
Boston, MA 02208

- - - - - - - - - - - - - - - - -

Enclosed is $_____ for the following books. (Add $1.00 postage when ordering just one book; if you order two or more, we'll pay the postage.)

_____

_____

_____

_____

_____

☐ Send a free copy of *Talk Back!* as offered above. I have ordered at least three other books.

name: _____

address: _____

city:_____state:_____zip:_____

ALYSON PUBLICATIONS
Dept. B-52, PO Box 2783, Boston, Mass. 02208

This offer expires Dec. 31, 1986. After that date, please write for current catalog.